A Woman of Honor; A Child of God

by
MeLissa Ann Ross

Bloomington, IN  Milton Keynes, UK

AuthorHouse™
1663 Liberty Drive, Suite 200
Bloomington, IN 47403
www.authorhouse.com
Phone: 1-800-839-8640

AuthorHouse™ UK Ltd.
500 Avebury Boulevard
Central Milton Keynes, MK9 2BE
www.authorhouse.co.uk
Phone: 08001974150

This book is a work of fiction. People, places, events, and situations are the product of the author's imagination. Any resemblance to actual persons, living or dead, or historical events, is purely coincidental.

© 2006 MeLissa Ann Ross. All rights reserved.

No part of this book may be reproduced, stored in a retrieval system, or transmitted by any means without the written permission of the author.

First published by AuthorHouse 3/17/2006

ISBN: 1-4259-2279-1 (sc)

Library of Congress Control Number: 2006902020

Printed in the United States of America
Bloomington, Indiana

This book is printed on acid-free paper.

Dedication

To God be the glory. This book is dedicated to my family, who supports me in all that I do. Whether it is Writing, Singing, or Preaching, you're always there to encourage me, and for that I am eternally grateful. Thanks Ray, and kids, Mom, Dad, and the rest of you! Couldn't name you all or that would be another book. To my wonderful proofers, I couldn't do this without you.

This book was written with the Christian Teen/Young Adult in mind. In a time when peer pressure can be an overwhelming creature, I urge you to stay true to yourselves, and the Word of God. In the end only what you do for Christ shall last. Just because everyone else is doing something, it doesn't mean that you have to follow their lead. Stand for what you know is right, and true, even if it feels like you are standing alone. Remember God will never leave nor forsake you. You are never alone!

I BESEECH you therefore, brethren, by the mercies of God, that ye present your bodies a living sacrifice, holy, acceptable unto God, which is your reasonable service. And be not conformed to this world: but be ye transformed by the renewing of your mind, that ye may prove what is that good and acceptable, and perfect, will of God.Romans 12:1-2

With the Love of Christ,

Rev. Melissa Ann Ross

In Loving Memory

In, loving memory of PFC Wilfred D. R. Bellard. Will, as we simply called him, lost his life in the war with Iraq, at the tender age of 20 years old, but he will live on in our hearts forever. He was a young man dedicated to the notion of providing for his family. He is our hero, an example to both young and old of what true love is all about. Love is about sacrifice; it is unselfish, it is patient, and longsuffering. Will, out of love for his family, and his country sacrificed all, and for that we'll be eternally grateful.

PFC Wilfred Davy Russell Bellard, Child of God Father, Husband, Son, Friend, Soldier, and HERO!

In Loving Memory

In, loving Memory of Mrs. Judy G. Brown. My Judy as I affectionately called her, was one of my original three proofreaders. Many, was the day when she would call and urge me to write. She was the antidote to writers block. Although she is no longer with us in person, she's with us in spirit. We'll love you always My Judy, because after all, Love is Forever.

Chapter One

It was late and Angie knew that her parents were already asleep for the evening. Without hesitation she picked up the receiver and dialed Tommy's number. Tommy answered on the second ring, "Hello", "It's me", she replied. "What took you so long to call me back?" he asked.

"I had to wait until my parents went to sleep, you know they don't allow me to use the phone after 11pm."

"Man yo parents treat you like a kid". "Come on lay off my parents Tommy, they just want to make sure that I get enough sleep, so I can keep my grades up." "Speaking uh grades you gon work on my English report for me baby." "Ah Tommy why can't you do it this time, I'm working on a report for Ms. Reed's class that's due on Friday."

"Ah come on baby, you know I got ball practice everyday, and when I git done wit dat me and da fellas hang out a lil bit." Sighing she answered, "Ok Tommy I'll do the best I can, give me all the details tomorrow." "That's my girl, hey when we gon git together and do a lil sumpum, sumpum? You keep promisin a brother an thangs."

"I told you Tommy I'd like to take my time before we move to that." "Yeah but you didn't say it was gon be this long baby, na listen, if you gon be wit me, you gotta show me you love me, much as I love you."

"Ah Tommy you know I love you." "Well I'm jus saying it ain't enuff for me."

"But Tommy you said you'd wait until I was ready." "Well what ya think I been doin girl? We been on for about three months now and we ain't knocked the boots once." "Soon Tommy I promise soon we'll be together." "Yeah whatever, you said that weeks ago."

Disappointed in the direction of their conversation Angie simply said, "Well I guess we'd better say goodnight, I love you Tommy."

"Yo wuz up wit dat, every time I talk about us taking care of each others needs you ready to hang up?" "It's not that Tommy, really, I'm just starting to get tired is all."

"Whatever, later."

"Aren't you going to say I love you too, Angie?"

"You just said it for me, bye." Click he hangs up the phone before she could make a comment. Angie fought back tears as she settled into her bed, she quickly said her prayers and fell asleep just as lone single tear rolled to the surface of her pillow.

Tommy, after hanging up with Angie decided to call one of his other girls. Monique answered after the third or fourth ring, "Hello."

"Bout time you answered girl, what took you so long to git to da phome?"

"Yo son wuz jus going ta sleep, daz what." "Oh, I wuz jus calling to see if a brother could come ova fuh a lil while daz all." "Na you know you ain't gotta call me to come ova here Tommy, wuz wrong wit you?" "Nuttin, I be da in a few." "Alright", replies Monique and hangs up. She wakes up her younger sister and tells her to go sleep on the sofa, because Tommy was coming to spend the night. The child sleepily walks to the sofa dragging a sheet and a pillow sucking her thumb. Monique pushes little TJ over to the corner of the bed that meets the wall to make room for Tommy and herself. She then goes to the kitchen to unlock the door for him. She passes by her mother on the way to the kitchen who asks in a heavily slurred voice, "Yo man coming huh, I see ya made yo sista move out ta da sofa."

"And, what about it?" asked Monique. "Betta not let him gie ya a nutta one, ain't doing nuttin for da furst one", came her mother's reply.

"Ain't nobody tryin ta hear all that, I don see you wit no man." Glancing over while waiting for a reply she noticed that her mother had nodded off as addicts often did, while on a high. Hearing approaching footsteps she opened the door and greeted Tommy with a welcome hug and kiss. Touching her breasts through the oversized T-shirt she had on, Tommy kissed her greedily and whispered how much he wanted her. Together they strode to the back bedroom and begun to undress each other and make love on the same bed as their sleeping nine- month old son.

Sluggishly Angie turned off her alarm clock and slowly got out of bed. She could already hear her mother in the kitchen readying breakfast and making her father's lunch. She quickly showered and dressed and went downstairs to greet them.

"Good Morning", she called out. Smiling her mother wiped her hands on her apron and said, "Good Morning sweet pea, Dad will be down soon. " Set the table, and pour each of us a glass of orange juice." "Sure Mom."

"Well Good morning to two of the most beautiful ladies in all the world," came her father's reply from the doorway. Both turned to smile and greet him. They ate quickly and left for work and school. Angie waved goodbye to her father as he pulled out of the driveway and walked to the bus stop where she met up with her best friend Tomeeka. "Hey girl, that some new jeans," called out Tomeeka. "Yeah, I hope Tommy likes them replied Angie smiling hopefully. "Girl you need to stop worrying about Tommy and start thinking of yourself sometimes." "I'm thinking about myself," replied Angie.

"Oh no here comes Hoochie I and Hoochie II," Tomeeka said as she noticed two other girls coming to the bus stop. A'quanetta and Nicole strode up to wait for the bus all the while laughing and giggling about something their friend Monique had told them about her boyfriend. Upon spying Angie and Tomeeka they called out a greeting and stood off from the gathering crowd so they could continue to trade tidbits of gossip. Angie and Tomeeka shook their heads and wondered what could be so interesting to the two girls but soon forgot them entirely as they boarded the bus and headed for school.

Ms. Reed asked a question and was now awaiting an answer, she had apparently called on Angie to give an answer, but for the life of her Angie didn't know how to answer it, because she had been reading a note from Tommy she found stuffed in her locker. Tapping her foot impatiently Ms. Reed cleared her throat and said, "Angie is that note something the whole class would be interested in or would you rather give it to me and let me decide." "Uh no ma'am replied Angie." "To which question are you referring to Angie," inquired Ms. Reed. "To both of them Ms. Reed", said Angie and placed the note in the back of her notebook.

"I would suggest then that you pay attention in class young lady or next time, I will simply remove the note from your possession and see for myself." "Yes ma'am", replied a sullen Angie.

Later while walking to 5th period, Angie was met by Tomeeka who demanded to know what was wrong with her.

A Woman of Honor; A Child of God

Angie told her about the note she got from Tommy and waited for the statement she knew would come from her friend.

"If I told you a thousand times, I'll tell you again girlfriend, you need to find you a man who respects you." "Tommy respects me Meeka and don't start in on me ok." "Then why is he always fronting you in front of his friends, and calling you his…" Interrupting before Tomeeka could finish, Angie said quickly, "He doesn't front me and he just likes to tease me that's all."

"Well if he was my man he wouldn't be treating me like that, besides you could have any man you wanted, why him?"

"Look Meeka I don't tell you how to run your relationship with Lance so don't try to tell me about Tommy and me."

"Look girl I'm just trying to help you that's all, so what did the note say."

"Nothing he just wants to talk to me that's all."

Unconvinced Tomeeka asked once again, "Are you sure that's all."

"Yeah that's all, now lets get to class before we're late", said a now smiling Angie.

The two girls walked briskly to their next class, one wondering what her friend's note had really said, the other wondering how to get over the shock of what the note contained. The girls entered the classroom and took their seats, Tomeeka in front of Lance, and Angie in front of Tommy. Angie sat quietly in front of Tommy without meeting his gaze and occupied herself with writing the heading of the lesson, this now more than anything alerted Tomeeka that something was definitely wrong, and she made a mental note to herself not to rest until she found out what it was.

Angie could barely wait until the end of class so she could escape the watchful eyes of her friend. She tried desperately to concentrate on what was being taught, but found that no matter how hard she tried her attention wandered to last line of the note...

I can't wait much longer baby to feel yo body next to mine. Besides if we keep it on the down low, who will know but us. Meet me after practice in the old gym, or fogit bout bein my woman.
Tommy

Finally to the relief to Angie the bell rung and signaled an end to the class. She left the class without glancing back at her friend or Tommy, who were both puzzled by her behavior. Determined to help her friend, Tomeeka turned to Tommy and demanded to know what was in that note.

"Listen to me Tommy Boy, you tell me what you've done to upset my friend and be quick about it,"

"Yo hold up, you better stay outta my bidness", man you need ta git yo girl in check", he stated as he turned to face Lance. Without waiting for an answer he sauntered off to his last class of the day.

Angie gulped a breath of fresh air once she was out of the building, and hurried to the gym for PE and dressed out for class. She quickly formulated a plan to get out of exercising and subsequently cheerleader practice. Slowly she made her way to where the girl's coach was seated and gave her a rather convincing story. Just as she had hoped, she was told to sit quietly on the bleachers for the next hour and to go home directly after school and not to bother with cheerleading practice until she was feeling better. Angie was elated that her plan had worked so well, now she had no doubt that Tommy would believe her when she told him that she couldn't meet after practice because she had been sick. Everyone knew that you couldn't fool Ms. Jordan; she was as sharp as a tack.

"Angie, honey it's a friend of yours from school, a Tommy somebody or another." Called her mother from the family room door. "Ok momma," replied Angie. Answering the telephone she said, "You can hang up now momma I have it." "Hi Tommy, I was waiting for your call."

"Yeah I had ta tell yo moms I was yo science partna", chuckling he added, "pretty good huh."

"I suppose so", was all she said.

"So wuz up wit you anyhow babygirl, how come you wuz acting so strange in class ta day?"

"Yeah, I wasn't feeling too hot, but I think I'll be much better on tomorrow." "I sho hope so, then we ken spend a lil time together before da game, hey you workin on dat report fa me?" "Yes, I'm almost done with it just one or two more paragraphs and it'll be ready." "That'll work, by da way, wear a skirt tomorrow, easy access, know what I mean." "Ok Tommy." "Hey how comes you don sound as happy as I am bout dis here." "I'm happy it's just that I'm not feeling well again, I'll see you tomorrow, Goodbye Tommy."

Not waiting for a reply she hung up and rolled over onto her back and felt more miserable that she had when she gotten his note earlier. She knew she had to make a decision by tomorrow if she wanted to continue being with Tommy, he wouldn't wait forever. Angie had been taught all her life that sex before marriage was wrong, and she'd never questioned the concept until she'd met Tommy and fallen madly in love. Tommy said that adults just said this so their children wouldn't grow up too fast, could Tommy be right? After all her daddy was always saying that his baby was growing so fast it made his eyes hurt. Maybe Tomeeka could help her out; surely she and Lance were involved sexually. She put on her shoes and ran down the stairs, calling out to her mother that she'd return in a little while. "Just make sure you're home before nine

Angie", called her mom. Looking down at her watch Angie realized she had about two hours to figure this thing out before returning home.

Chapter Two

Tomeeka was out on the porch with a couple of other girls from the neighborhood that Angie didn't know, and felt a little disappointed that she wouldn't have Tomeeka all to herself for a while. "Hey girl looks like you're feeling better", said Tomeeka.

"Yeah I guess I was just a little tired."

"Well I'm glad you came over we were just talking about you and Tommy."

Puzzled by this announcement, Angie asked, "Why were you talking about us."

One of the other girls Angie didn't know giggled and said, "We was just wondering if you and Tommy was gittin busy is all, I mean we all know you go ta church and everythang."

Offended Angie said a little more sharply that intended, "Tommy and I are just fine and that's all you need to know." Tomeeka realizing that this could turn into something physical quickly jumped in to say, "Lay off my girl, Nika." Changing the subject she turned everyone's attention to Lela Dobson the new girl in the neighborhood. "Hey yall look at the newbe, lets go say hello."

The other girls got up to follow her across the street. Angie however lagged behind with her thoughts solely on her problem. She was so absorbed in her thoughts that she didn't hear the call of watch out being heralded by an oncoming bicyclist headed straight for her. Without knowing what hit her, Angie awoke to see people standing all around her. She closed her eyes and gave her head a slight shake, trying to clear it of all the fuzziness. From a distance she heard her mother's worried voice asking if she was ok. Slowly she felt her body being lifted and being placed on some sort of bed. She gave in to the urge to fall asleep again and dozed off just as they were placing her in the back of the ambulance.

Angie awakened to a splitting headache and to the face of a nurse checking her vital signs. Trying to cushion her head in her hands she suddenly realized where she was but had no idea how she'd gotten here or why. Whispering she asks, "What happened, how come I'm at the hospital?" "Ah, so you're awake, how do you feel", replied nurse Halloway. "Like my head is going to split open at any moment", managed Angie. "Good, I'll notify the doctor that you're awake, and I'm sure your parents will be glad to know this as well." Leaving the room the nurse dimmed the lights again to help ease some of the pain Angie was feeling.

The door swung open almost immediately to admit her worried parents. Rushing to her bedside they ask anxiously, "How are you baby?" "Fine mom, dad." Before they could exchange any more dialog in comes the attending doctor and asks everyone else to leave while he conducts an examination of the patient. "Well young lady how are you feeling", he asks. "My head hurts real bad, what happened?" Holding open her left eyelid he asks, "Are you nauseous or is your vision blurry?" "Yes sir to both questions", mumbles Angie. "Well

A Woman of Honor; A Child of God

I'd say that you took quite a blow to the head and I would have been surprised to hear you say that you weren't experiencing any symptoms consistent with a concussion." "A Concussion, what happened", asks Angie again. "Well the report says that you were hit pretty hard by a cyclist while crossing the street in your neighborhood." A small " oh", was all Angie could manage. Placing a hand on her arm the doctor said before taking his leave, "We'll keep you here and run tests for a few days, try to get some rest." Stepping into the hall, he informed her parents of her condition. "Well Mr. And Mrs. Hill, It looks as if your daughter has a concussion along with a few other minor injuries, her arm is bruised, but not broken." "I will keep her here for a few days for observation and then release her."

Extending his hand her father shook the doctor's hand and expressed his gratitude. "Thank you doctor for all you've done.

"No thanks necessary Mr. Hill, I'll speak with you all again tomorrow morning while making my rounds."

"Goodnight doctor", replied her parents. Watching the doctor walk down the corridor they made towards the door to Angie's room and entered quietly.

Later that evening while at Prayer Meeting, the "Prayer Warriors", prayed for Angie's recovery. Her mother dabbed away tears as the Pastor led them in prayer for Angie, along with the rest of the teens of the Christian House of Praise Worship Center. After service concluded, Mr. And Mrs. Hill gave Pastor Jenkins Angie's hospital room number, and left with the assurance that He would go to visit her on tomorrow.

Driving home Mrs. Hill said softly, " Thank You Lord, I feel so much better now, I'm so glad we didn't miss Intercessory Prayer tonight."

"Well He does say come unto me, all ye that labor and are heavy burdened, and I will give you rest", answered Mr. Hill.

"Yes He does, and now I'm a living witness that He'll do just that", his wife replied while placing her head against his shoulder. He patted her hand and drove towards their home, thanking God silently for His grace and mercy.

Chapter Three

"Girl you scared the life out of me", came Tomeeka's voice. Laughing along with her friend, Angie replied, "Hello Meeka." Placing her hands on her hips, Tomeeka feigned anger by shaking her finger and saying, "Don't you hello Meeka me, I nearly lost my mind when that biker ran you over."

"Sorry about that, I guess I just wasn't paying attention."

"Fess up Angie, it's that knucklehead, Tommy, again isn't it?" asked her friend. Shrugging her shoulders Angie didn't answer but instead looked out of the window. Moving towards the bed Tomeeka took her hand and stated, "Listen to me girlfriend, Tommy is a nobody, and you deserve better."

"Not now Meeka", replied Angie. Trying to steer the conversation in a different direction she suggested that Tomeeka tell her about what had going on at school for the last couple of days. "Hey what's been going on in Ms. Reed's class this week?"

Not fooled for a minute Tomeeka said, "You ain't fooling me Angie, I know that Tommy is the reason you didn't see that guy on the bike."

"Meeka, I don't want to talk about Tommy ok." Gasping Tomeeka said, "He hasn't even been to see you has he?"

"Girl you gotta cut that lowlife loose, Angie he don't care nothing bout you. All Tommy wants is what you can do for him."

Both girls stopped speaking and watched as Angie's parents enter her hospital room. Forcing a smile on their respective faces, the girls greet them warmly. "Hello, Mr. And Mrs. Hill, I just stopped by to check on Angie."

"Hello Tomeeka", answered Mrs. Hill. Turning to her daughter she said while placing a kiss upon her brow, "Hello, sweetheart, how are you feeling today?" Moving to stand in the spot just vacated by her mother, Mr. Hill bent and placed a kiss on her cheek as he said, "Hello, darling, good to see you looking so well."

"Hi Mama and Daddy. I'm doing great. In fact the doctor says that I can go home tomorrow."

"Yes we know, we just saw him on his way out."

"Hey that's just wonderful Angie", exclaimed Tomeeka. "Yeah, just in time to turn in that book report for Ms. Reed's class", responded Angie.

"Silly girl, just because you're coming home, doesn't mean that you're ready to return to school", her mother said while laughing softly.

"Besides", chimed in Tomeeka, "I bet old Ms. Reed will give you an extension or something."

"Don't worry so much about school sweetie, I've already spoken with all of your teachers. You won't be responsible for turning in any assignments until you are able to return to school", stated her father.

"Whew, that's a relief. Thanks Daddy", she replied.

"No problem baby girl, and now your Mother and I will go home and prepare your room, is there anything special you'd like for us to pick up?"

"Nothing that I can think of Daddy. Thanks and I'll see you tomorrow morning."

"Goodnight sweetie", her mother said as she walked to the door. Turning back she glanced in Tomeeka's direction and said, "Make sure not to stay too long Meeka, Angie needs to get some rest, Ok."

"Sure thing Mrs. Hill, I'll only stay a moment longer."

"Ok, Goodnight girls."

Watching her parents leave, Angie dreaded what she knew would come next. Although their conversation had been interrupted she knew that her friend would pick up right where she'd left off.

She didn't have long to wait as she heard Angie ask, "Tommy hasn't been here has he?"

"He probably doesn't even know I'm in the hospital Meeka, give him a break."

"What?" "Girl you tripping, Mr. Moore announced it over the PA during Homeroom."

"Ok, so he knows, he's probably busy with practice for the big game on Friday night."

"Angie, stop making excuses for that duck."

"I'm not Meeka, really, he'd come if I asked him to."

"I do not believe I'm hearing this. Angie you shouldn't have to ask him to come over, he's your boyfriend remember."

"Look, Tommy and I have a different type of relationship than you and Lance. He's probably waiting for me to call him right now."

Trying to prove her point, Tomeeka walks over to the phone and hands it to Angie. "Well call him."

"Meeka", started Angie.

"Call him", Tomeeka commanded as she patted her foot impatiently against the floor.

Angie dialed the number slowly and waited for someone to answer. One, two, three rings went by until she finally heard a voice on the other end. "Hullo."

"Hello, is Tommy there", she asked tentatively.

"No he ain't here", answered the person on the other line. "Could you tell him that Angie called?"

"Yep", was all she heard before the person placed down the phone.

She handed the phone back to Tomeeka and said, "He's not in."

"Tsk, I wonder who he's running a game on tonight?" asked Tomeeka.

"Meeka", said Angie warning her to back off and drop the subject.

"Ok, well you just get some rest, and I'll drop by the house tomorrow after school", Tomeeka promised.

Smiling sadly Angie said, "Ok, and thanks for coming by Meeka."

"Hey, you know you my girl", replied Tomeeka as she picked up her backpack and headed for the door.

"Yeah, I know, but thanks anyway. I'll see you tomorrow afternoon."

Angie lay back against the pillows and let her thoughts roam over what Meeka had said about whom Tommy was with tonight. Did he really see other people besides her? No, Tommy said that he loved her, Meeka just didn't understand. He was most likely hanging out with the guys or something. I mean if he were really seeing other girls someone would have said something by now, wouldn't they? She dozed off still thinking about Tommy.

Waking up around eight, she decided to give it another try and dialed his number once again. After being told that he was still not in she decided to watch some television and try to reach him a little later.

Glancing at the clock she noticed that it was ten fifteen and dialed the number one more time. This time his mother answered and informed her that Tommy was not in, hadn't been in for two days, and was not expected in, any time soon. His mother even went so far as to suggest she try calling at his girlfriend's house. "Try calling round there to that Adams' girl's house, you know they got a baby together."

"Yes Ma'am", she replied.

Placing the receiver down quickly, Angie dashed away the tears spilling over her lashes. Turning onto her side she cried her heart out and vowed that she and Tommy were over. Oh God how could she have been so gullible. A baby! Tommy had a baby with another girl. Why hadn't he told her about the baby, why had he kept it a secret? Why hadn't Meeka said anything about Tommy and this Adams girl having a child together? She just couldn't believe it. Tommy had another girlfriend and a baby. Everything he'd said had been a lie, had it all been just a scheme as Meeka claimed?

No, Tommy loved her, just as she loved him, maybe he hadn't told her about the baby because he wasn't sure how she'd react to the news. Yeah, that was it, no way could she bring herself to believe that Tommy didn't really love her. She was sure that once he explained things, everything would be all right. Resolving to give him a chance to clear things up she fell asleep cradling one of her pillows.

Looking up as the door opened and closed, Tommy's mother said while putting down the receiver, "That was for you. Some young lady been trying to reach you all evening."

"What, all evening, who could that be?" asked Tommy conceitfully.

"Some young lady by the name of Angie, talks real proper like."

"Angie, what did you tell her mama?"

"That you wasn't here, and hadn't been here for two days. Told her to call down to that Adams girl's place."

"You did what, Ah mama that's whack." "Ah man, now what I'm gon do?" he asked aloud.

"What cha mean by that?" asked his mother suspiciously. "You haven't been stringing this girl along have you boy?" "And you better not tell me she's pregnant too."

"No mama, ah man you don messed everything up", he said in response to her statement. Turning serious eyes towards her son, his mother said, "She sounds like a real nice girl Tommy, you better not get involved with her, cause you got responsibilities now, you're not free boy."

"Yeah, whatever."

Moving to grab his chin in her hand his mother said angrily, "Don't you whatever me boy, you got one baby already, and still got to finish school."

"Don't worry Mama, me and Angie just friends, she helps me wit my work is all", he lied smoothly.

"I'm warning you boy, I know what you up against", his mother warned.

"Ah Mama, things gon be better for me, cause I'm a man, sides I'm gon git dat scholarship playing football at da college."

"Don't count your eggs before they hatch son. What if something happens and you don't get that scholarship?" asked his mother.

"Stop worrying Mama, nothing ain't gon happen, I got scouts coming tomorrow night to watch me play."

Giving her a quick hug he plucked an apple from the counter and said Good night as he went to his room. "Good night Mama."

"Night son", she answered over her shoulder and hoped that her son was being straight with her.

Chapter Four

Angie sat back and relaxed as her father drove them home from the hospital. She listened as her mother chatted on and on about what had been going on at church all week. "Mrs. Abnie will be singing a solo this Sunday. She's singing Amazing Grace as the hymn of preparation."

"Wow, I don't want to miss that", Angie said while rolling her eyes heavenward. Laughing her father said, "Yeah, we should really be in for a treat."

"Ok you two, what matters is that she desires to sing for the Lord, not how it sounds", reminded her mother.

Mr. Hill looked at his daughter through his rear view mirror and promptly burst into laughter as she struggled to keep a straight face. Finally able to hold it in no longer Mrs. Hill also gave in to the laughter bubbling inside. Wiping away tears of mirth, she finally managed to say through her laughter, "Father, forgive us." The three of them laughed the rest of the way home. Her parents helped her into bed and left her with instructions to take a nap until lunchtime. "Just rest honey, I'll bring you up some soup at lunch and help you downstairs for a couple of hours."

"Thanks Mom", answered Angie as she snuggled under the soft coverlet. She was asleep before her father turned off the light and shut the door.

"Well I'm off to the office for a couple of hours honey. I'll be home early tonight", Mr. Hill said as he placed a kiss on her cheek. "Go on we'll be fine babe", she replied.

Tomeeka sat fuming as she watched Tommy getting busy with one of the girls from the pep squad. How dare he treat her friend Angie like this? He hadn't even bothered to visit her once this week, and now here he was all up on Shelia Watson.

Walking up to the unsuspecting couple she said, "Hey, Tommy how are you? You know Angie is out of the hospital. Are you going over after school?" She delighted in the fact that Tommy looked as if he wanted to wring her neck.

Forcing himself to remain calm he said, "Hey Tomeeka, matter of fact I was going to visit her later after practice."

Looking from one to the other Shelia picked up on the unspoken vibes and said, "Look I'll catch ya later Tommy."

"Now hold up", he replied. Holding up her hand she stated, "No, I'll see you later, I gotta go." Watching her walk away, Tomeeka nearly burst into laughter at the look of utter frustration on Tommy's face. Turning to face his nemesis Tommy could have sworn that for just a moment he'd seen a smile. Looking her squarely in the eyes he said as sternly as he could manage, "Look here, you need to quit actin so shiesty."

"Oh, I'll chill alright, as soon as you leave Angie alone", retorted Tomeeka.

"I'm only gon say dis one time and one time only, what I do wit Angie ain't got nuttin ta do wit you."

Furious almost beyond reason, Tomeeka yelled, "That's what you think duck, but I know better."

"Duck! You calling me a duck?" yelled Tommy. Just then Lance and a couple of the other players from the basketball team walked up on the scene. Stepping in front of Tomeeka he asked, "What's up Tommy, there a problem?"

"Yeah, yo girl can't mind her own bidness." Pointing towards her he says, "You better stay outta my way."

Stepping forward Lance says, "Yeah well just so you know, her bidness is my bidness, you gotta problem with my girl, you got a problem with me." Thinking twice about tackling Lance and his buddies, Tommy backed down and said, "Jus a misunderstandin, we cool dawg."

Once Tommy was out of earshot, Lance turned and took Tomeeka by the arm. Moving a little ways off from his friends he said, "What was that all about?"

"Nothing, he just didn't like it that I was concerned about Angie is all."

"Listen Meeka, I know Angie's ya girl and all, but don't you think she's old enough to handle her own bizness?" he asked.

"Not when it comes to dogs like Tommy, she doesn't have a clue", answered Tomeeka.

"Yeah, well leave Tommy alone, talk to Angie, but leave him be", advised Lance. Pulling her into his arms he kissed her and then suggested she get a move on before she was late for cheerleading practice.

Knock, knock, knock. Looking up Angie called out, "Come In."

Tomeeka, Ashley, and Felicia all walked in and greeted her. "Hey girl, how you holding?" asked Ashley as she took a seat next to the bed.

"Aw, I'm ok, how are you guys?" responded Angie.

"We doing just fine", answered Felicia.

Angie watched as the other two girls looked at Tomeeka who in turn looked away. Knowing that something wasn't right Angie asked quickly, "What is it, what's wrong Meeka?"

"I had a run in with Tommy today, Angie" replied a reluctant Tomeeka.

"What?" "What kind of run in", asked Angie?

Moving to sit on the other side of the bed Tomeeka said, "Stay calm Angie, it was nothing really, just a misunderstanding," replied Tomeeka.

"Misunderstanding my behind, tell her the truth girlfriend," answered Ashley.

"Yeah, Meeka, give her the 411" added Felicia.

Turning confused eyes towards her friend, Angie said softly, "Tell me the truth Tomeeka, what happened with Tommy today?"

"I got in his face and he just responded, but everything is ok now", answered Tomeeka.

Sitting up Angie asked, "What do you mean, you got in his face, and why Meeka, what happened?

Not wanting to upset her friend Tomeeka tried to downplay the incident to the snorts of Felicia and Ashley. "Well I told him to stay away from you and he got a little angry."

"You did what?" cried Angie aloud. "How could you do something like this Meeka? "I thought you were my friend."

"Angie I am your friend that's why I did what I did", Tomeeka replied.

Shaking her head from side to side Angie said, "No, a friend wouldn't interfere like this, especially if asked not to. I can't believe you betrayed me like this Meeka."

Ashley, having heard enough of this nonsense spoke up by saying, "Listen Angie you need to know the truth."

Trying to dissuade her Tomeeka interrupted by saying, "No Ashley, don't."

Not to be deterred, Ashley gave her a look that said a girl has to do, what a girl has to do. "Girl please, Tommy is a lowlife and Angie deserves better." Turning to face Angie she said, "Angie girl, Tomeeka was doing you a favor. She caught Tommy all up on Shelia Watson today and they wasn't just talking either."

Looking to her friends for an explanation Angie asked, "What do you mean, what were they doing?"

When no one answered her question she turned to look at Tomeeka and said, "Tell me what you saw Meeka."

Hearing the despair in her friend's voice, Tomeeka took a deep breath and said slowly, "I'm not sure but it looked like they might have been kissing."

"Not sure" shouted Felicia. "Girl, you better tell her the truth or I will," she stated angrily.

When Tomeeka hesitated, Ashley took that as her cue that someone else was going to have to tell Angie what they all knew to be the truth. Stepping forward she looked at her friend with sympathy before telling her exactly what Tommy and Shelia had been doing. "Angie, they were getting busy right there in the gym near the bleachers by the back showers."

Unable to hold back the tears Angie cried while her friends gathered closely around the bed and cried with her. "I'm sorry Angie, I'm so sorry", Ashley said as she wiped away tears spilling onto her cheeks.

"Listen girl you are smart, beautiful, and got everything going for you, forget Tommy", Felicia pleaded through her tears.

"I can't, I can't, I love him so much" Angie said while crying.

Holding her friend in her arms Tomeeka spoke up by saying, "I know Angie, I know how you feel about Tommy but girl he doesn't feel the same way about you."

"No you're wrong, he loves me. He says so all the time. Besides this is all my fault", Angie argued.

"Your fault! Shouted and outraged Ashley. "Girl please! Stop the drama! Tommy's the one who's been lying and cheating, not you."

"Listen to me Angie, Tommy's only using you to do his homework so he can stay on the team," said Felicia.

"No, you're wrong he does love me. It's just that I haven't, that is, we haven't…" Angie said groping for the right words.

"You haven't what?" asked Ashley.

"They haven't had sex yet", supplied Tomeeka.

"So what, neither have AJ and me, but you don't see him chasing everything with two legs and breasts", answered Ashley.

"Hold up, put on the brakes, what you mean, you and AJ ain't getting busy?" asked Felicia.

"Just what I said. He respects my decision to wait until marriage", replied Ashley.

Truly intrigued by this turn of events Angie sat up and asked, "Is this ok with him, Ashley?"

"Ok? Listen girlfriend AJ loves me enough to respect my wishes, and doesn't pressure me about doing otherwise."

"You mean he just accepts your view and doesn't question your love for him?" Angie asked curiously.

"Yeah, whether we have sex or not has nothing to do with our love for each other", responded Ashley.

Chapter Five

Felicia spoke up next by saying, "Angie not all guys are like Tommy. Mitchell and I are also waiting until we're older."

"No way", laughed Ashley.

"But, but I thought that everyone was doing it. At least that's what Tommy said", came the reply from Angie.

"That's what we've been trying to tell you Angie, not all guys are like Tommy. And no not everyone is doing it", this coming from Tomeeka shocked them all.

Seeing the stunned looks on her friend's faces she laughed and said "Lance and I haven't exactly done it either."

To this announcement all the girls promptly lost themselves to a fit of giggling until they were now wiping away tears of mirth. They laughed and talked for over two hours of what was going on at school, and who was and wasn't doing the do. After all of the laughter finally died down Tomeeka looked at Angie and asked, "Are you sure you're ok Angie?"

"Yes, I'm ok and thanks you guys for this afternoon", she said sincerely. Gathering their backpacks and standing to leave the girls each said goodbye and promised to stop by for another visit later this week.

Once she was alone in her room, Angie let her mind wander to the thoughts of all she and her friends had discussed earlier. She wondered if she'd ever love anyone else they way she loved Tommy. She knew now that it was over between the two of them, besides Tommy hadn't even bothered to come by or call to check on her. Tomeeka had been right all along about his motives, why hadn't she listened? Well, no need to cry over spilled milk. Resolving to move on with her life she put Tommy out of her thoughts and settled down for a nap before her mother came in with dinner. Just before dropping off to sleep she whispered a prayer for God to guide her and show what she should do. She fell asleep while still praying.

After the longest week in history, Sunday rolled around, and just as her mother promised, Angie watched as Mrs. Abnie stood near the piano and began to sing the Hymn of Preparation. In her squeaky first soprano voice, the older woman opened her mouth and sang, *"Amazing Grace, how sweet the sound, that saved a wretch like me. Oh oh oh oh oh oh oh oh… I once was lost but now I'm found, was blind but now I see,"* Finally when it seemed as if she'd sang every verse, Pastor Jenkins entered and made his way to the pulpit.

Finding his text he thanked her for that beautiful rendition of the favorite hymn and proceeded to dive right into his sermon. "Thank You Sister Abnie for that beautiful rendition of Amazing Grace. Surely you will agree with me that it was simply soul stirring to say the least." Angie coughed to hide a snicker as her father whispered, "Don't know about Soul Stirring, but my ears were certainly stirred up."

She stood along with everyone else as the Pastor began to read from 1 Corinthians 1-20 verses. She moaned inwardly as he read the verses about fornication, and knew that she was in for another lecture about no sex before marriage. She visibly sat lower in her seat as she heard him say, *"Young people refrain from fornication because your bodies are temples of the Holy*

A Woman of Honor; A Child of God

Spirit. And know this right now that the Holy Spirit cannot dwell in an unclean temple. Your bodies are not your own, but belong to God so that he can live within you, Do I have a witness this morning?" On and on the sermon went about how you should conduct yourself as a Christian, and how you should resist the temptations of the flesh. Finally the hour-long minute sermon was concluded, the choir rose to sing, "Come unto Jesus."

Walking out of the church Angie took in a deep breath of fresh air as her father left them on the front steps to while he went for the car. "You're awfully quiet Angie, are you feeling ok?" asked her mother.

"I'm fine mom, just a little tired that's all", replied Angie. Concerned her mother turned to look fully at her and said, "Maybe you shouldn't return to school for a few more days, I'll call the doctor as soon as we get back home."

"No, Mom, really I'll be fine. I need to go back to school, mid terms are coming up."

"All right sweetie, but only if you feel you're up to it", her mother stated firmly.

Pulling up in front of them, her father got out and came around to open their doors. After settling them in he returned to the driver's seat and headed home. "That Mrs. Abnie was sure in fitting form today, huh, baby girl?" he asked with laughter crinkling the corners of his eyes.

"Ha ha ha ha ha ha ha," the laughter bubbled up and out before Angie could control it to her mother's protestations.

"Stop it Martin, what kind of example are you setting for Angie by talking about Sis. Abnie's singing?"

"Singing? Is that what you call it?" he asked playfully. "For a moment I thought a cat had gotten loose within the sanctuary", he continued before bursting into laughter with Angie over the apt description. Unable to restrain the laughter herself, Mrs. Hill soon joined in and laughed at her husband's antics.

Later that evening while sitting up reading the last chapter of her American History assignment the phone rang. Picking it up on the second ring she wasn't prepared for whom she heard on the other end. "Hello", she said.

"Angie, yo, what up baby girl?"

"Hello, Tommy, what do you want?" she replied.

"What cha mean what do I want? That ain't no way ta talk ta yo man girl", he answered.

"No Tommy you're not my man, not anymore."

"Girl you tripping, it's that Tomeeka girl huh", he asked guiltily.

"Tomeeka? Who said anything about Tomeeka?"

"Well the only one don't like me, and always filling yo head wit stuff is Tomeeka."

"Tomeeka cares about me Tommy which is more than I can say for you."

"Girl you know I lul you. Tomeeka jus jealous, and she ain't yo real friend, neither."

"You're wrong Tommy, it's you who isn't really who you claim to be."

"What cha mean by dat?" he asked impatiently.

"What I mean Tommy, is that you've been playing me all this time, just to get me to do your homework so you could stay on the team."

"Girl, do you know how many of dem chicken heads want what you got? They all wanna git wit me, but they know you my girl."

"And how about Shelia Watson, is she in your fan club too, Tommy?" asked Angie.

"See, dere I knew dat Tomeeka was gon run and tell you bout dat."

"So you admit that you were with Shelia?"

A Woman of Honor; A Child of God

"Look all Tomeeka saw was Shelia trying ta get at me, but I turned her down baby, cause I wanna be wit you." "Girl I lul you so much, I can't even think straight. I can't sleep, I can't eat, all I think about is you."

Angie, who until that moment had been sure that she wanted nothing more to do with Tommy, felt her heart do a little leap at his words and claims of love for her. At the silence on the other end Tommy pressed his suit further by saying. "C'mon baby you gotta believe me, I don't lul nobody the way I lul you. "You da first woman I ever lul dis way, and you gon be da last."

"Tommy, I…"

"Baby listen, nobody make me feel da way you do." "I lul you Angie like I ain't never lul nobody befoe."

"C'mon say you lul me too Angie." Unable to fight the feelings any longer Angie gave in and told him what he wanted to hear.

"I love you too Tommy."

"Good girl, I'm gon see ya at school tomorrow?" he asked.

"Yes, I'm returning tomorrow", she said quietly. "Good cause I don know how much longer I could go wit out seeing ya baby."

"I've missed you too Tommy."

"What I really missed wuz holdin ya in my arms, and kissin ya."

"Really Tommy? Have you really missed being with me?" she asked tentatively.

Feeling elated that he now had her convinced of his feelings for her, he said, "Girl I miss ya so much till I dream bout cha at night." "I'm telling ya girl you all I ken think about."

"Sometimes I have dreams about you also Tommy."

"Yeah, what kind of dreams?"

"You know, about us being together", she said shyly.

"I dream bout us being ta gether too, you and me gitting busy, doing a little sumpin sumpin." "Sometimes I wake up in a sweat girl, dreaming bout you and me."

Giggling Angie glanced at the clock on the wall and noticed that it was nearly nine o' clock and said, "I wish I could talk longer but I have to go now."

"Alright, I'll see you at the school tomorrow, I lul ya girl."

"I love you too, Tommy, bye."

After hanging up Angie hugged herself and reveled in the feelings washing over her. She had been almost sure that Tomeeka had misunderstood what was going on between Tommy and Shelia, now she knew it beyond a shadow of a doubt. Tommy had called her and told her how much he loved her. Believing Tommy's response to have been her answer from God, she whispered a prayer of thanks and snuggled deeply in her covers falling fast asleep.

Chapter Six

Angie couldn't wait to talk to Tomeeka at the bus stop and tell her of the conversation she'd had with Tommy last night.

"I do not believe this", declared Tomeeka as she listened to her friend go on and on about Tommy and how much he loved her. "Angie surely you don't believe all that nonsense Tommy told you?"

"Nonsense? He was being honest Meeka; he loves me. And you said yourself that you weren't really sure about them kissing."

"Angie girl, I just didn't want to hurt your feelings. But I'm sure they were kissing, in fact they were doing a lot of bumping and grinding along with the kissing."

Tomeeka was shocked at what Angie said next, because in all their years of being friends they'd never even remotely had an argument.

"Maybe Tommy is right, you're jealous of our relationship."

"What, Oh you trippin now. Whatever Angie", holding up her hand as if to say talk to this, she walked away to board the bus.

Angie entered the bus and sat near the front and was soon lost to her thoughts. She was just so confused; she didn't know whom to believe. Was Tommy really as bad as her friend said or was the problem really Tomeeka. Could her friend just be envious of her because Tommy was the most popular boy in school, and she ,Angie Hill, was his girl? I mean everybody knew that he had offers for football scholarships from four different colleges. Was it really envy? Her head began to ache as the thoughts swam round and round. Finally the bus pulled into the front drive of the school and true to his word; Tommy was there, waiting for her.

Stepping down she walked right into his arms as he greeted her with a kiss in front of everyone. This convinced her more than anything that he really was sincere in his affections.

"Mornin boo", he said when the kiss ended.

"Morning Tommy", she answered.

Making eye contact with Tomeeka over her head he said loudly, "Who luls ya baby?"

"You do Tommy", Angie replied as he wrapped his arm around her and led her away from the bus.

Watching them walk into the building Tomeeka cringed and made her way to find Felicia and Ashley so she could inform them of the latest. She couldn't believe that Angie would accuse her of such a thing. It was all Tommy's fault, she just knew it with every fiber of her being. Somehow he'd convinced her friend that he was innocent of all wrongdoing, and that everybody else was lying.

Spotting their friend walking into the building with Tommy, Felicia and Ashley stood with their mouths open and sought out Tomeeka for an explanation. Spotting her they asked simultaneously, "Girl what's up with Tommy and Angie?"

"Well as you can see, they're back together", replied Tomeeka.

"No way, I don't believe this, how did he convince her to take him back?" asked Ashley.

"I don't know but I'll tell you what else, talking to her won't do any good", supplied Tomeeka.

"Why not?," asked Felicia.

"Because somehow he has her believing that I'm jealous of their relationship and want to break them up for my own selfish reasons."

"Stop the drama!" exclaimed Ashley.

"Yeah girl, this morning matter of fact she tells me that Tommy says I'm just jealous because I want what she has."

"No she ain't trippin like that", stated Felicia.

"Oh yeah girlfriend she trippin, and trippin hard over that duck", Tomeeka said as she walked down the corridor to homeroom with her two remaining friends.

Angie watched as one by one all of her old friends chose a different table and refused to sit near her at lunchtime. She sat and listened as they all spoke gaily about the day's activities without once looking her way. With her appetite suddenly gone she emptied her tray and made her way out to the courtyard. She made up in her mind that if that's how they wanted it, that's how it would be. If they no longer wanted her friendship she didn't want theirs. She took out the rough draft of Tommy's book report and re-read it to make sure that there were no mistakes. Thinking of how he'd openly greeted her this morning brought a smile to her face. After making a few minor adjustments to the report it was finally time to go to fourth period. At the sound of the bell she put away her books and walked to her locker. On the way she spied Tommy and several of his friends in the hallway. She walked over to where he was standing and nearly stumbled in shock as she heard Terrence ask Tommy about Shelia Watson.

Spying her Tommy played it off by saying, "Hey man what's up wit dat, trying make my girl break up wit me or sumpin?" Laughing it off the fellas watched as he motioned for Angie to stand near his side. "It's all cool dawg I was jus messin wit cha", Terrence replied.

"It's all good bro, all good, she know she my one and only", said Tommy. Leading Angie away towards their fourth hour class he called to the fellas over his shoulder that he'd see them later.

"Hey don let them fools git ta ya, now", he said while pulling her in for a smack on the lips.

"I won't Tommy", came the reply.

"Dats my girl", he said while winking.

Chapter Seven

"Martin, something just isn't right. Tomeeka hasn't called for Angie once this week", Evelyn Hill said to her husband.

Looking up from his newspaper her husband said, "Sweetheart, you know how kids are, they're probably just having a disagreement about something. I'm sure that the girls will work out their differences in no time at all."

"I hope you're right, but I just can't shake the feeling that there is something big going on", she stressed. "Well, if you feel that strongly about, why don't you go up and speak with her", Mr. Hill replied while once again glancing at the paper. Giving the idea her full attention, Mrs. Hill finally decided to do just that. Leaving the kitchen she said, "I think I'll do just what you suggested, Dear, be right back." Not bothering to look up he waved a hand in her general direction and murmured a simple, "Ok, Dear."

Walking up the stairs Mrs. Hill pauses at her daughter's door as she hears her speaking over the phone with someone. Turning on her heel she went back down to the kitchen. Upon her entrance Martin looked up and asked, "Done so soon honey?"

"She was on the phone and I didn't want to interrupt her, after all she may very well be speaking with Tomeeka", said Mrs. Hill suddenly brightening over this thought.

"Exactly, so stop worrying those two always work out their differences", he replied with a smile.

"You're right. I 'm probably just getting all worked up over nothing". Turning she sets up the coffee pot and asks, "Care for a little coffee, I've got tea cakes."

Setting down the paper with a frown he says, "Tea cakes, boy you're really worried about Angie aren't you." "What? No, I mean why would you say that", she asked while taking two saucers from the cupboard.

Laughing lightly he said, "Sweetheart, whenever you bake it's a sure sign that something is troubling you."

"Martin, you know me better than I do myself at times" she replied.

"Hey, I'm your soul mate remember, I 'm supposed to know when something's going on with my other half", he responded. As she moved to place the saucers with the teacakes on the table in front of him, he reached out and took her hand into his. Placing a small kiss on the palm he said, "Sweetheart, listen we've raised her right, if she is having a problem trust that she'll come to us."

"You're right, thanks Dear", she answered.

With a puzzled look creasing his forehead he asked, "Thanks? For what darling?"

"For always knowing the right thing to say when I'm concerned about something", came the reply.

Upstairs on the phone, Angie was talking to Tommy about his report. "I'm almost done, as a matter of fact, I was just typing the last two paragraphs", she told him.

A Woman of Honor; A Child of God

"See, dat's what I'm talkin bout. I'm gon git it from ya in da mornin."

"I'll have it with me. Make sure you're waiting for me, like you were today, ok", she answered.

Laughing he said, "So you liked dat huh."

"Yes, I like the idea of you waiting for me first thing in the morning", came the shy reply.

"Yeah, but I bet yo girl Meeka ain't too happy bout us makin up", he asked.

Feeling weighted down by his comment, Angie shrugged and spoke with false bravado, "I don't care if she's happy or not about us, I don't tell her what to do with Lance, and I'm not going to let her tell me who I can see."

"I'm feeling ya baby. Just make sho you don't let hur fill you head wit nothin", he answered.

Trying to reassure him she spoke up by saying, "Don't worry Tommy she won't, I Love You and now that I know you care about me too, nothing's going to keep us apart." Hearing her parents coming upstairs she quickly concludes the conversation and says, "Well I have to go now, I'll see you tomorrow, Tommy."

"Yeah alright baby girl, I'll see ya in da mornin."

"I Love You, Tommy", she said quickly

"Me too", Tommy replied and then hung up. Putting the phone on the desk she moved back to the computer and looked up as her father rapped softly and then opened the door.

Looking in he said, "Still at it sweetheart?"

Rubbing her tired eyes she answered, "I'm almost done dad, I had a lot of catching up to do."

"Ok, but not too much longer, almost time for bed, and if need be, I could send a note to your instructors and ask for more time."

"Oh no Dad, that won't be necessary, in fact this is the last of the missed work", she said nervously.

"Good, cause you need your rest, you're still not a hundred percent yet", came the concerned reply.

"Ok, Dad goodnight, are you guys going to bed now", she asked.

"Yes", came the reply as her mother now peeked in from the doorway.

"Goodnight Mama", Angie answered.

"Night baby, are you sure that you don't need anything, before we turn in", her mother asked.

Shaking her head no Angie said, "No, nothing, I'm fine, in fact I'll be turning in myself in just a few minutes.

"Good", her parents said in unison and then laughed quietly. Looking back at their daughter they said their goodnights and closed the door gently.

Watching them leave Angie breathed a sigh of relief and returned her attention to Tommy's report. Putting on the finishing touches she hit the spell check and once finished set up the printer. After making sure that it was printing ok, she took out her pajamas and headed for the shower.

Chapter Eight

True to his word, Tommy was there waiting for her as the bus pulled onto the school grounds.

Angie smiled sadly and stood as the bus pulled to a stop. Her mind was still in a whirl of confusion after the awful confrontation she and Tomeeka had just had at the bus stop. She had ridden to school in total silence after the bombshell dropped by her ex-friend about Tommy. "Thought you'd like to know Tommy's a daddy", Tomeeka had said to the chorus snickering of some of the other students standing nearby. Unwilling to let them all see the shock rifling her, she had replied with a humping of the shoulders by saying, "That's old news to me Meeka, Tommy and I have no secrets." At this Tomeeka had been shocked along with everyone else that Angie knew about Monique and the baby. She came back to the present as she walked slowly off the bus.

"Mornin Sunshine", Tommy said as she stepped down.

"Morning Tommy", she said as she plastered a fake smile upon her lips. Although her lips were smiling her eyes were laden with tears as her heart felt as if it were cracking in two. Tommy noticed the slight trembling of her bottom lip and asked, "What's up baby girl."

Stiffening her back and holding her head high Angie said, "Nothing, let's go."

Puzzled at her behavior Tommy wrapped his arm around her tiny waist and walked away, leaving their fellow classmates to stand and stare after them. When they were inside the building and halfway down the hall, Angie turned to Tommy and asked, "Why didn't you tell me about the baby?"

"Baby, what baby?," came the shocked reply.

"Your baby, Tommy why didn't you tell me?" Angie asked on the verge of tears. Searching his mind for an explanation that would placate her, Tommy finally had one that sounded plausible to him.

Taking a deep breath and bringing his gaze up to look her in the eye, he said as shakily as he could manage, "Cause I thought you'd leave me if you knew." Pausing for effect he waited and then explained further. "I didn't think you'd be wit me knowing I gots a kid, I mean you go ta church and all dat."

Hearing his explanation, her heart did a small somersault. Softening towards him once again she lifted her hand to his cheek and said, "I'm sorry, I should have realized that Meeka was just trying to push my buttons."

Breathing a sigh of relief he forged ahead as to put the icing on the cake, "Baby girl I don want ta lose ya fa nuthin in dis world.

"Don't worry, you won't lose me, just no more surprises ok", she stated feeling much better now. She shrugged off the memory of his mother once saying something about a baby.

"Awright no more suprizes", he said as he moved in close for a kiss while making a mental note to have a little talk with Tomeeka.

"So?," asked Ashley anxiously.

A Woman of Honor; A Child of God

"So what?," asked Tomeeka in reply. Throwing up her hand Ashley says while sweeping Felicia with a quick glance, "What happened when you told Angie about Tommy's baby?"

Placing her hands on her hips in annoyance, Tomeeka, blew out a frustrated breath and said, "What do you think happened Ashley?"

"No, say it ain't so", Ashley replied.

Shaking her head Felicia spoke for the first time by saying, "I'm afraid so, she said she already knew, and that she and Tommy don't have any secrets between them."

"What? Girl that's a bunch of bull and you know it", Ashley replied with anger threatening to snuff out her every word.

"But what if she's telling the truth?" asked Tomeeka uncertainly.

Shaking her head in denial Ashley presses forward by saying, "No, I don't believe for a minute that Angie knew anything at all about Tommy's relationship with Monique."

"I'm with Ashley on this one, but then again why would she lie?" asked Felicia.

Weary of the whole situation, Tomeeka shook her head and said, "I don't know, I just don't know anymore Fe". Turning to face Ashley she said while heading for the building, "C'mon guys lets get to class. The three walked into the building with each of their thoughts on their friend and her situation. As they entered the locker hall, whom did they see, but Tommy and Angie kissing in full view of everyone.

Rolling her eyes heavenward Ashley says loudly, "Great just what my already upset stomach needed."

Laughing Felicia joins in and says, "I'm with cha there girlfriend, matter of fact I don't really need anything from my locker, I'll see ya later."

Watching her walk away, Tomeeka finished getting her books out for the first four periods and said to Ashley, "Let's go I have all I need."

Without sparing Tommy and Angie another glance the two walked off towards their homeroom.

Breaking the kiss, Angie says breathlessly, "We'd better make it to class, I think I just heard the bell ring."

"Yeah, let's go", Tommy said as he led her towards homeroom. After reaching the doorway he asked quickly, "Hey you got my report?"

"As a matter of fact I do", she said as she dug through her backpack. Pulling it out and handing it to him she lifted her lips for another kiss.

Obliging her, Tommy took the report with his free hand and kissed her once again. Ending the kiss he pointed her towards the door and said, "Let's go or Ms. Smith's gon mark us tardy."

Murmuring that he was probably right Angie walked into the classroom and had just taken her seat in front of Tommy as the tardy bell rang loudly.

Chapter Nine

Finally it was Friday night and everyone was feeling the excitement of having scouts present at the high school game. The coach took time before the game to speak with his team and try to calm their jitters by reminding them of what tonight would mean for three of his senior players.

"Listen up guys, just go out there and play your game, and we'll be victorious. Remember to play as a team, no showing off or spotlighting your talents. These guys want to see how well you can play as a team member. Don't let them or yourselves down by doing something stupid." When he'd looked each of his star players in the eye and gotten confirmation that they understood his message he moved to stand in the center of the players. Standing tall he stretched out his hand and said loudly, "**ONE FOR ALL AND...**" **and** smiled broadly as echoes of **"ALL FOR ONE"**, filled the locker room of the field house. When they all had been pumped up, they exited and began to make their way towards the ball field to the cheers of the community.

As captain of the squad, Tomeeka moved forward with the other members to stand near the goal posts and hold up the banner that read, *Lakeside Pirates are #1,* in black and gold painted letters. Angie made eye contact with Tommy as he lined up to take his place. Winking he watched as she blushed and shyly winked back. Stepping up he positioned himself to run through the banner. As he ran through he reveled in the elation at hearing them all cheering and calling out his name as he ran onto the field. Making their way across the field and over to the sidelines, the team waited as the captains walked onto the field and greeted the other team captains. They watched as the coin was flipped and it was in the Pirates' favor. Opting to receive they ran back to the sidelines and received instructions from Coach Garrett. "Ok, lets go return team. Make sure that Matthew gets set up to run it back", he yelled while clapping his hands. Everyone waited while the opposing team set up the kick and the kicker began running towards the ball. As soon as his foot made contact with the football everyone began yelling for their team. Catching the ball, Matthew ran and dashed to the left as a hole was opened due to a good block by a teammate. He managed to advance all the way up to the forty- yard line before being tackled to the ground. Before going out onto the field the offensive line got last minute instructions and then ran out onto the field.

Angie cheered all the more as Tommy took his place as Quarterback, behind the center.

Lining up the squad faced the audience and began to rouse the crowd in support of their team.

"C'mon team let's go, hey c'mon team lets go", clap, clap, clap. They continued the chant until the crowd was repeating it loudly. Turning around to catch the play they cheered on as Tommy handed the ball to the running back. They watched as he made his way to the fifty-yard line, gaining the necessary yardage for a first down. Cheering loudly the girls advanced down the sidelines to cheer from this section. As the team took up their positions, the girls began the next chant, "Fired, Fired up, Fired up to win."

A Woman of Honor; A Child of God

Once again Tommy handed the ball off and the running back gained yardage, however this time he was four short of the first down. Setting up again, they watched as Tommy ran back and prepared to put the ball into the air. At last he got the ball off and the split end made a clean catch. Running he got a good block from one of the tackles and made his way towards the opponents ten-yard line. The crowd roared its approval. Running back to get more instructions, Tommy listened as the coach called for an additional tail back to enter the lineup. Running back to the formation he quickly gave them the play and set it up for execution.

The girls began the cheer, "What do we want TD, what's that Touchdown", and turned around to watch the play. The cheering was monumental as the running back made it across the goal line to give the Pirates an early six-point lead on their first possession. After the PAT, the scoreboard read Home 7, Guest 0.

Later on their third possession of the ball their opponents scored their first touchdown making it a tie game. The Pirates had failed to score on their other possessions, and now it was time for the second quarter to begin. The girls cheered crazily hoping that their team would score. Finally with there only being two minutes before half-time Tommy took the ball and ran it in himself. The crowd went wild with exhilaration as their team scored seven more points making the score 14-7. Cheering as the team went back to the locker room for a break, the girls decided to do the same. Pairing up they each went to the concession stand for drinks and a quick snack. Angie chatted happily with Anessa, one of only two cheerleaders still on friendly terms with her. Paying for her chili pie she turned as she heard her name being called, and nearly fainted when she spied her father making his way towards her.

"Dad, what are you doing here?" she asked.

Smiling broadly he said, "Thought we'd catch the big game honey, I even talked your mother into coming tonight."

"Oh, wow, how'd you manage that?" she asked while looking around nervously hoping that he didn't ask about Tomeeka.

"Promised to go to the movies on tomorrow night and watch anything she'd like to see", he said with a chuckle. Before she could answer however, up walked Tomeeka, Ashley, and Felicia.

"Hello, Mr. Martin, how are you?" asked Tomeeka.

"Fine, and just how are you young ladies this evening?" he replied.

Sucking in her breath Angie waited silently as Tomeeka and the others traded pleasantries with her father. Such hypocrites, how dare they stand there and talk with her father, and speak to her only when it was absolutely necessary. Sorely tempted to confront them right then and there she stopped as suddenly another thought leapt into her mind. Oh God, what was she going to do now? She was supposed to meet Tommy after the game; tonight they had made plans for…

"Angie?" she heard her father said with concern writ on his handsome face.

"I'm ok Dad", looking around she noticed that the other girls are making their way back to the field to watch the marching band perform. "Look, I'd better go Dad, see you after the game", she said before dashing away.

Shaking his head her dad says aloud, "Teenagers". Still chuckling her walks back towards the bleachers, and hands his wife her watered down coke before saying, "I just saw that lovely, confusing daughter of ours at the concession."

"Oh great, does she know to meet us near the field house after the game?" she asked.

"Darnit, I forgot to tell her that we'd parked there instead of our usual place, I'll go down and tell her right now, before the half starts", he replied.

Making his way down to the lower level of the bleachers he calls out "excuse me", over and over until finally he's at the bottom. Leaning over the rail he calls for Angie to come forward, but couldn't be heard over the cheering of the crowd as the team made their way back onto the field. Deciding to try later, he walked back to his seat and said, "Too late, but don't worry, we'll find her after the game."

The third quarter was just as exciting as the first with the home team scoring on their first possession of the ball. The crowd cheered them on as play after play the Pirates seemed to be in control of the game and on to a solid victory.

Coach Garrett called for the I formation on their next play and watched with satisfaction as the team executed the play almost to perfection. He had given them a pep talk during the break and tried to keep them in the right frame of mind. It only took one or two to get the big head and their victory would dissolve before their very eyes. He had to admit though; Tommy was leading the team like a pro. Turning his attention back to the game he frowned as one of the Guards limped back into the huddle. Coach Garrett quickly called for a timeout and had the team doctor examine big Willie, the injured player. He looked towards the bench and called for a replacement. "Ok Wilkins, you'll be in for Big Willie. Let's see what you got." Placing his helmet on his head Wilkins ran excitedly on to the field. Coach Garrett turned his attention back to the game while the team doctor examined Big Willie for injuries. He watched with excitement as his team moved their way up the field towards the end zone with precision. The crowd roared their appreciation as Tommy fired off a long one down the field, and it was caught by the receiver bringing them within ten yards of the end zone. Excitement bubbled from every nook and cranny of the stadium. Angie and the others cheered until they sounded as if frogs had taken residence in their throats. Momentarily the girls forgot their differences and embraced as their team scored another touchdown. Falling into formation the girls chanted, "Lakeside Pirates are number one, hey Lakeside Pirates are getting it done." Angie moved into position to be lifted up atop the pyramid. The crowd clapped loudly as she was hoisted up, and then did a back flip to begin her descent. Her mother covered her eyes and said against her husband's shoulder, "Oh Martin my heart stops everytime they do that cheer." Chuckling he said, "You can look now she's back on her feet dear." "Thank God" she said as she clapped wildly along with the other spectators. The crowd turned their attention back to the field as the game progressed to the fourth quarter. The Pirates were relentless in their quest for a victory and wowed the fans with two more touchdowns. As the last seconds ticked away the cheering was nearly deafening. With the last second gone the winning team rushed the field hugging one another and shouted victoriously. The cheerleaders ran as well, each greeting their favorite player.

Chapter Ten

Angie ran towards Tommy and laughed happily as he picked her up and swung her around. He kissed her and whispered, "don forgit ta meet me later, baby girl."

"I may be a little late, my parents came tonight", she rushed to say as he put her down.

"Just don leave me hangin, you betta be by the locker room", he warned as he turned to celebrate with his friends. Angie ran back to the sidelines to gather her gear and quickly made her way towards the parking lot. She just had to find her parents and let them know she'd be staying for the victory dance in the gymnasium. Just as she went through the gate her father called her name.

Turning left she smiled and headed towards him saying, "Dad I was just looking for you guys." "Oh yeah, and why would you be doing that young lady", he asked while smiling.

"Well, I've decided to stay for the celebration dance in the gym", she answered.

"Uh oh", he said shaking his head, "I think we'd better run this by your mother." Walking with him she sighed and hoped that her mother would let her stay. Approaching the car she smiled brightly and quickly asked, "Mom, there is a victory dance in the gym tonight, can I stay"

Thinking to object her mother began by saying, "Now Angie you know we don't approve of you being out so late but, I guess if Tomeeka and the others are staying …" Not giving her mother the chance to ask, Angie hugged her quickly and said, "Thanks Mom." Next she turned to her father kissed him slightly on the cheek and ran towards the gym, waving goodbye.

Driving home her mother let out a small sigh and looked out of the car window. Hearing the sigh her husband remarked, "Stop worrying dear she'll be fine, besides after what she's been through recently, she deserves to have a little fun." Smiling softly Mrs. Hill answered, "Yes she does, you're right again, it's just, oh I don't know, something just doesn't seem right Martin."

"What doesn't seem right dear", he asked while pulling into the driveway. "That's just it Martin, I don't know exactly, it's just a feeling that something is going on that Angie isn't telling us."

"Sweetheart, I'm sure that all is well with Angie. Relax a little, we've raised her right, she can handle herself, replied Mr. Hill. Pulling the car into the garage, Mr. Hill got out and came around to open his wife's door. Leading her inside he suggests that they take advantage of their time alone, "Look at it this way, we have a couple of hours to ourselves", he said while raising an eyebrow. "Martin, honey are you suggesting what I think you are", Mrs. Hill answered while smiling. Taking her into his arms he said huskily, "And you're smart too."

Stepping away he says, "Go on upstairs and I'll lock up down here."

Looking back over her shoulder Mrs. Hill replies, "Don't be long, Martin."

"Five minutes and then I'm on my way", he answered while loosening the collar of his shirt.

A Woman of Honor; A Child of God

Angie waited outside the locker room for Tommy to arrive while looking around nervously. Beginning to fidget she looked up to see a young woman with a baby on her hip waiting on the other side of the entrance. Smiling timidly she asked, "How old is your baby."

"Six months came the reply." If she expected anything more she was sorely disappointed. The young woman returned to playing with her baby without giving Angie a second thought.

Just then one of Tommy's friends, Big Willie came out of the locker room and upon spying both Monique and Angie outside he dashed back inside to inform his friend.

Nearing knocking Tommy down, he says excitedly, "Yo man don walk out dat door right now, Angie and Monique are both waiting for ya."

"What, aw man, look, tell Angie ta meet me at the gym, I'll take care of Monique", replied Tommy as he tried to think of what he would say to Monique. "Aw right dawg, see ya later", said Big Willie.

Angie looked up as Big Willie came out and walked towards her, "Hey Tommy wants you to meet him at the gym, he's going to be a while", he said quietly.

"Why, what's the problem, he's not hurt or anything is he", she asked.

"No, nuthin like dat, he just needs ta talk ta coach, dats all", replied Willie. Convinced that he's telling the truth, Angie allows Willie to lead her towards the gym. Monique watches them walk away and chuckles to herself, "Go big Willie."

Watching Big Willie and Angie from the window, Tommy waited until they were out of sight before going out to greet Monique.

"Hey baby girl, what's up", he asked as she handed him his son.

"Nuthin, just thought I'd congratulate cha fa a job well done, daz all", Monique answered. Moving in a little closer she puckers up and kisses him before stepping back to look up into his eyes.

"Yo mama out ta night" he asked inquiringly as she began to walk away. Shrugging nonchalantly she said simply, "You know mama."

Angie checked her watch again; it had been over twenty minutes and still no Tommy. She decided to walk towards the entrance, glancing at the gym once more and not seeing him, Angie went back inside. Big Willie and the others watched as she did this three more times. Finally when he could take no more Big Willie went over to her and asked, "Would you like me to walk you home Angie, I don't think Tommy's gon make it."

"But Willie, didn't he say to meet him here", she asked with puzzlement marking her features.

"Yeah, but, Angie he'd da been here already, if he was gon come", Willie explained gently. Not willing to give up hope Angie shook her head stubbornly and said, "No it's only been a hour, maybe he and coach are discussing his scholarship offers." Shaking his head once more, Big Willie walked away and went to join his friends.

"Well what did she say", asked his friend Jason.

"She still waitin on him", answered Willie.

Shaking their heads the two walked off towards the concession stand to buy a soda.

Angie glanced down at her watch a few more times and then finally realized that he wasn't coming. How could Tommy do this to her? Why hadn't he shown up? Looking around to see if anyone noticed that she was alone Angie proceeded towards the exit. Glancing around one last time through eyes shimmering with tears, she left the gymnasium.

Big Willie watched as Angie left the building. Saying goodnight to his friends he walked quickly after her calling her name, "Hey Angie wait up, I'll walk you home."

Turning to face him Angie started to refuse then thought better of it and slowed her pace allowing him to catch up to her. When he was beside her she said simply, "Thanks Willie."

"You're welcome Angie", was all he say. The two walked slowly towards her house without speaking. Each lost to the jumble of feelings threatening to consume them. Angie's heart was breaking in two, and she fought desperately to keep the tears from falling down her cheeks. Meanwhile Willie was fighting to keep his anger at Tommy in check. He knew that if Tommy were present he'd probably strangle him with his bare hands. How could Tommy do this to someone like Angie? I mean Angie was a princess, smart, pretty, and decent. He made up his mind to let Tommy know just how he felt about his treatment of Angie.

Reaching her front door, Angie again turned to say thanks and wish Willie goodnight. Conjuring up a smile that didn't reach her eyes she said half-heartedly, "Thanks Willie and have a goodnight. I'll see you on Sunday."

"Yeah, I'll see you at Church, and Angie don't…, Goodnight Angie", he said before turning and walking away.

Angie let out a breath of relief; she knew that if he'd said one thing about Tommy, that the tears would fall without restraint. Entering the front door, she locked it softly and went upstairs to her bedroom. There she could let the tears fall unchecked and maybe, just maybe the constriction around her heart would ease enough for her to breathe a deep breath or two.

Chapter Eleven

Entering her bedroom quietly, Angie locked the door, turned on the television and fell onto the bed. Taking her pillow with her she curled into a ball, and cried her heart out. Careful not to make a sound she held the pillow to her face and cried until she was gasping for air. Why had Tommy done this to her? She was sure that everyone was laughing at her behind her back. Without a doubt that's all they would be talking about, how she was Tommy's special fool.

"Why Tommy, why", she whispered in the dark. She fell asleep with the question still burning a hole in her brain.

She slept late the next day, mainly because she wasn't up to answering the questions she knew her parent's would have about the dance. Finally when her stomach began to groan so loud that she could no longer ignore it, she dressed and went downstairs.

Her mother and father were in the family room watching a Saturday matinee from the sound of things. Making her way to the kitchen she put on a cheery face and said, "Hey, you two catching a movie I see."

Turning towards the archway her parents smiled in greeting. "Good to see you up, thought we'd have to go up and get you", replied her father.

"Don't mind your father Angie, I made chicken salad if you're hungry", said her mother.

Patting her stomach, she asked while laughing, "How'd you guess Mom"

"Mothers have an extra sense about those things baby girl", quipped her father.

"Do any of you guys want anything", she asked.

"No you go ahead baby girl, we just had popcorn", said her mother.

Sniffing the air Angie said, "the smell is probably what woke me up."

Angie went to the kitchen and took out the chicken salad and toasted some bread. Going to the cupboard she took out a bag of plain chips, her favorite, and poured a tall glass of apple juice.

As the toast popped up she placed the bread onto the plate and began to spread the salad thickly onto the slice. Hearing the phone ring she put the knife down and called out, "I'll get it Mom."

"Hello", she answered.

"Hey baby, what happened to you last night", asked Tommy from the other end.

"What do you mean what happened to me, where were you", she asked angrily while trying to keep her voice down.

Calling from the other room her mother asked, "Who is it Angie"

"Uh, its for me Mom", came the reply.

"Make sure you eat Angie, tell them you'll call them back", her father said from the family room.

"Ok, Dad", she said and returned to the phone call.

"Tommy I've got to go, I'll have to call you later", Angie said as she followed her father's instructions.

"Awright, I'll be waitin fur ya call", said a quiet Tommy.

Hanging up Angie took a deep breath, and glanced towards her sandwich, suddenly it was no longer as appealing as it had seemed just a moment ago. Not wanting her parents to become suspicious and start asking questions, she ate what to her now tasted like sawdust. Finishing up Angie moved to the sink and washed her plate and glass. Walking back to meet her parents, she yawned loudly and said, "Think I'll take another nap, guess staying out so late doesn't agree with me huh"

"Angie are you feeling ok", asked her mother, suddenly concerned that her daughter may be doing too much after the accident.

"I'm just a little tired Mom, that's all", Angie replied.

"Well we were going to take a drive over to the mall but if you're not feeling up to going out, we'll just stay in", her father added.

"No, by all means please go. I'll be just fine, besides you guys need a little time out together", Angie suggested hurriedly.

"Are you sure baby girl, I mean we don't have to go out", her mother stressed again.

"No Mom really, you guys go out and have a good time, I'm just going to take a nap and get a little reading done", Angie offered as a reply.

"Ok, then it's settled, she'll get some rest and we'll go out for a while", stated Mr. Hill.

Angie kissed each of them goodbye, locked the door, and then went to her room.

Her mind was in a whirlwind. What had Tommy meant, by where was she? He was the one who'd left her to her own devices last night. Well if he thought he could talk his way out of this one, he was mistaken. Taking a deep breath, she picked up the receiver and dialed his number.

"Hello", came Tommy's voice over the line.

"Hi, Tommy, it's me, Angie."

"Baby, what happened, I…" Interrupting Angie said hotly, "Don't give me that Tommy, I waited for you nearly two hours."

"Look, I had a meeting with coach and a scout, didn't Big Willie tell you", asked Tommy.

"Yeah but…" Pouncing in quickly Tommy said, "Well, things ran a little longer than expected, but I did cum by ta scoop ya up."

Rushing forward before she could get a word in or have a chance to think too clearly he added quickly, "Girl, you know you mean da world ta me, I wouldn't do ya like dat." Feeling her heart melt at his words, Angie allowed a smile to break through.

"I'm sorry Tommy, I just jumped to the wrong conclusion. When you didn't show up I thought maybe you were with someone else", she explained.

"With someone else? Girl dere ain't nobody else. You all I care bout Angie", Tommy said with what he hoped sounded sincerely.

"Hey ,who luv's ya girl", he asked sexily.

"You, do Tommy", came the reply.

"And don't cha forgit it", he added for good measure.

With her hopes once again restored, Angie said, "I won't Tommy, I Love You too."

"Dats my girl", was all he said in return.

"Oh by the way, we're having a Teen fellowship down at the church tomorrow, would you like to go with me", asked Angie.

A Woman of Honor; A Child of God

"Aw man, coach got me doing some extra practicing, maybe next time", he lied smoothly.

"Ok, maybe next time", she said trying to keep the disappointment out of her voice. In the three months since they'd been dating she'd invited him to church repeatedly. Although he'd said he'd love to attend with her, he'd never gotten around to doing it yet.

"Well I gotta hit the practice field, talk ta ya later", came his voice, breaking her out of her reverie.

"Practice field, You're working out today also", asked a surprised Angie.

"Yeah Coach, has me learning some new moves to help with the scouts", he answered.

"Oh, yeah, you did say that didn't you", she answered.

"Yeah, I did, you not listening, what's up wit dat", he asked.

"Just a little tired is all", Melinda said.

"Well git some rest, talk ta ya later", he said before hanging up.

Replacing the receiver she hugged her pillow to her. Once again she had misjudged Tommy, she would have to learn to trust him more. Too excited to sleep she got out of bed, picked up a magazine and tried to read about her favorite stars. Each time she turned to a new article she lost herself to the conversation she'd just had with Tommy. He really had gone to meet her, but she'd left before he arrived. She would have to simply learn to trust Him, and stop jumping to conclusions.

Hanging up, Tommy turned to face Big Willie and asked, "Now you happy, I talked ta hur."

Looking at his teammate with all the hate he could muster Willie replied with a sneer, "No I'm not happy, and won't be until you're out of her life."

"Well you'll be waitin a long time fa dat, my boy, cause I ain't letin hur go, no time soon", replied Tommy with a smug look written across his features.

Each took the other's measure as the two stared each other down. Fearing that the two would tangle, one the other players got in between them and said, "Hey come on Tommy, we gots thangs to be doin, man."

Taking a step back, Tommy says, "Yeah you right dawg." Walking away he makes one more comment to Willie. "Stay outta my mix Willie."

Chapter Twelve

Their classmates looked on as Tommy lifted Angie off the ground and kissed her soundly as she stepped off of the bus Monday morning. Many laughed and cheered them on, while a few like Tomeeka, Ashley, and Big Willie looked on in disgust.

Oblivious to their feelings, Angie relished in the fact that she was the object of Tommy's affection. Laughing gaily she said happily, "Good Morning Tommy."

"Mornin baby-girl", he said as he kissed her again.

Placing her feet gently onto the ground he led her towards the entrance while holding her hand tightly within his grip. He made to take the path that would lead them directly in front of Big Willie, and Tomeeka.

He laughed inwardly as he saw Willie tense up when he realized what Tommy's intentions were. In fact he nearly burst out laughing when he picked up the barely audible hiss Tomeeka couldn't contain as they swept past them on the front steps.

After making sure that they were out of earshot, Ashley muttered under her breath, "Sickening."

"Hahahahaha", laughed Felicia, adding, "Oh girl I know, they make me sick to my stomach."

"I'll second that", chimed in Tomeeka.

Furious that her friends were discussing her in this manner, Willie turned angry eyes on them and said sharply, "I thought you guys were her friends, with friends like you, she doesn't need any enemies."

They gasped in disbelief as he stalked away and down the steps towards the choir room.

"He's got some nerve", said Felicia angrily.

"Uh-oh, I think someone else has been bitten by the Angie bug", commented Tomeeka.

"What are you talking about now", asked Ashley with her hands resting on her hips.

"Come on you guys, surely you see what I see", Tomeeka said with a smile.

After receiving blank stares from her friends she answered, "Willie has a spot for Angie."

"What", shouted Ashley, "Girl you trippin now."

"No, No, I think she's right, I mean look how he watched over her Friday night, and he walked home when Tommy didn't show up", added Felicia.

"Now you feelin me", said Tomeeka.

"I have to admit that Willie and Angie sounds a whole lot better than, Tommy and Angie, and that would explain his behavior just now", commented Ashley.

"Question is, what are we going to do to help Angie see the light", asked Tomeeka with a mischievous twinkle in her eye.

The three of them laughed gaily and walked into the building, making their way towards the locker hall, finally they could do something to help their friend.

A Woman of Honor; A Child of God

Angie spied the note sticking out of her locker as she turned the corner. Smiling she took it down and opened her locker. It was fifth period and all she had was few moments before the tardy bell would ring. She collected her American Politics book and quickly unfolded the note. Her brow knitted in confusion, she re-read the note again. Angie had been sure that it was from Tommy, now she wasn't sure whom it was from.

Looking down she smiled as she read,

You are a diamond that outshines all others. If you were a star you'd be the brightest of them all. You are a prize among prizes. You are a princess without equal.
Signed,
Your Secret Admirer.

This had to be joke, surely no one would be admiring her from afar. Tommy was behind this no doubt. Spying him near the classroom door, she said, "Secret Admirer, huh."

Puzzled, Tommy just smiled and followed her into the classroom.

Angie waited for him to respond. When he didn't she jotted a quick note and passed it over to him while the teacher wasn't looking.

Tommy,
Did you leave that note stuck in my locker?

Looking at the note, Tommy shook his head no and wrote quickly, *No, what note?*

Unable to believe that Tommy didn't send the note she replied,

You know what note. The one signed Your Secret Admirer.

Reading what she had written, Tommy was suddenly furious. He had a feeling he knew just who the person was. Tommy made a mental note to confront his teammate at practice this afternoon. Turning his attention back to the matter at hand he responded by writing,

Naw it ain't me but I think I know who dun it. Gimme the note.

Angie read the request, but decided not to do as he asked. Shaking her head no, she moved it out of his reach as he tried to snatch it away. Just then Mrs. Hawkins turned around and caught him leaning towards Angie's desk.

"Mr. Ellison, what are you doing, may I ask?"

"I…I mean, I was uh…", Tommy stumbled around trying to come up with a valid excuse.

"Well", prompted Mrs. Hawkins.

"I was trying to see what you said last, ma'am", replied a sullen Tommy.

Placing her hands on her hips she stared at him under the rim of her glasses and said, "Yeah and I'm supposed to believe that right." Not waiting for him to answer she said, "See me after class Tommy."

"Yes, Mrs. Hawkins", answered a sullen Tommy.

Angie made sure to leave the classroom quickly after the bell rung signaling the end of fifth period. She hurried to her last class of the day before Tommy could catch up to her. She knew that he was furious with her for not handing over the note she'd found earlier. Her mind wandered back over the words she'd read. The person had said she was a princess, and one without equal to be exact. Who could have done such a thing? She had been sure that it had come from Tommy, but not now. Entering her gym class she went straight to the locker room and dressed out.

Tomeeka and Ashley were giggling when Angie walked in, and quickly sobered up as she walked towards them. "Hey Angie", called out Ashley.

Surprised that her old friend had called out a greeting Angie simply said, "Uh, Hi Ashley."

Wrinkling her brow in confusion she wondered to herself, what prompted Ashley to speak, I mean after all, her friends had all but abandoned her these last few months.

Ashley nudged Tomeeka slightly towards Angie and made a pair of eyes at her that said, say something, or I'm gonna…

"Hi, uh Angie, uh, how's it going", Tomeeka said clumsily.

Turning shocked eyes towards her two former friends, Angie replied, "Fine, why?"

"No reason, we were just wondering how you were", supplied Ashley.

"Yeah, that's it, we were just concerned about you, you know you being our girl and all", stumbled Tomeeka.

Laughing sarcastically Angie said, "Your girl, come on Tomeeka, until today, you hadn't spoken to me as a friend would in what, two, three, months. With friends like that, who needs enemies?"

Unwilling to let this turn into a mud slinging match, Ashley stepped around her friend and said contritely, "You're right Angie, we've been just awful to you, please forgive us."

Unsure of just what to say Angie looked at Ashley and then Tomeeka before saying, I…I don't know what to say, I mean, well…"

Placing her outstretched hand between them Ashley waited for Angie to either accept or reject the offer. Holding her breath she prayed, *Lord please let her accept this olive branch.* After hesitating for only a moment, Angie grasped her hand and said softly, "I forgive you Ashley."

The two hugged and laughed as they spied the tears welling up in the other's eyes. When Tomeeka could stand it no more she joined her two friends and the three of them rekindled their lifelong friendship right there in the middle of the Girls Locker room.

Chapter Thirteen

Tommy made his way to the Field house in search of Big Willie. He knew beyond a shadow of a doubt that it was Willie who had sent Angie that note. Well today, the big boy was gonna fall, and fall hard on the practice field. No one made a play for his girl, as boldly as Big Willie did, without paying the price. Slamming into his gear, he made his way out to the practice field in search for his target.

"Alright guys, first thing we're gonna work on is our I-formation. Let's line up and wait for Tommy to call out the play", instructed Coach Garrett.

Tommy got into position, called the play "End over right, 36, reverse at 9. He pivoted to the right, then turned to the left and pitched to ball to the tailback. Just as Big Willie set up to tackle Jones, Tommy hit him hard. Big Willie crashed to the ground with a thud, wondering what had hit him. Coach Garrett, came unglued, and called a halt to practice while the team doctor examined his linebacker. Grabbing Tommy by the shirt his voice shook with anger, as he demanded an explanation. "Just what the devil was that, Ellison?"

"I made the tackle coach, dat's all", offered Tommy.

Not buying his lame excuse for a moment Coach Garrett said, "Oh yeah, so you're a defensive man now. You got two seconds Ellison, speak up or get off of my practice field."

"But Coach, all I did wuz bring em down", Tommy tried desperately to explain.

Shaking with fury Coach Garrett, said in a voice booming like thunder in the heavens, "Off my practice field Ellison, and don't come back, until you're ready to be a part of this team."

"What, you ordering me off da field, fa Big Willie", Tommy asked in disbelief.

"Big Willie is one of the best linebackers this team has. This team has gotten this far on its hard work, not the work of one person, Tommy", answered Coach Garrett.

"But Coach, I got scouts coming again this Friday, and…", Tommy tried in vain.

"Boy I don't care if Edward Rozenburg, the commissioner of the NFL were coming, You will not play on this team, until you're ready to be a team player", fired back Coach Garrett, silencing any further objections Tommy could have made.

Stalking off the field, Tommy jerked off his helmet and made his way to the field house. Calming his breathing to a satisfactory pace, Coach Garrett turned his attention to his downed player asking, "How is he doc?"

"He's going to need to be examined further, Coach Garrett, I think we'd better watch him for a few days, to make sure that he hasn't suffered a concussion", answered the team doctor.

Bending down he asked Willie, "Son you know what this was about?"

Shaking his head no Willie stated, "No Sir, I don't have the slightest idea."

Noticing that Willie squinted as he gave the last of his answer, Coach Garrett ordered him to go with the doctor for further examination. "Go with the doc, son."

"Yes Sir", Big Willie answered as he moved off the field with the help of the team trainer and another of the team's players, suddenly his knees buckled and he collapsed. Barking out orders, Coach Garrett instructed one of the players to call 911.

A Woman of Honor; A Child of God

Later that afternoon while on the way home from Cheerleading practice Felicia ran up to Ashley and asked, "Girl did you hear what happened at practice today?"

"No what happened", asked Ashley. Moving closer so as not to be overheard, Felicia dropped her bombshell. "Rumor has it that Tommy and Big Willie got into a little something, something, and before it was all over, Big Willie had to go for x-rays at County General."

"What", yelled Ashley. "What happened, tell me the whole story, girl and don't leave out nothing."

"Well Mitchell says that today out on the practice field, Tommy hit Big Willie so hard that he couldn't move for almost 20 minutes girl, and that after all was said and done, the doc took Willie with Him, and Willie passed out cold. Coach had to call an ambulance and everything. Mitchell even said that Coach threw Tommy off the team", replied Felicia.

"Threw Tommy off the team, oh my God, but, what about Big Willie, I…I mean how's he", asked a worried Ashley.

Shrugging her shoulders Felicia says, "I don't know, Mitchell didn't say."

"I've got to find Meeka, this isn't good", said Ashley before running off to find her friend, leaving Felicia to ponder her last statement. Shaking her head to continued on down the lane towards her home shaking her head in puzzlement over Ashley's behavior.

Ashley hurried towards Tomeeka's house, with a sick feeling resting in the pit of her stomach. What if the note that she and Meeka had planted had caused Big Willie to be injured in some way? "*Oh God, she prayed, please let Willie be ok. Please don't let it be our fault that he's been hurt. We didn't*

mean for anyone to get hurt, just for Angie to look at Willie as more than just a friend. Oh God please, please..." she cried over and over in her mind. Hoping against hope that their prank hadn't provoked Tommy into hurting Willie.

Reaching Tomeeka's front door, she paused before knocking, praying once more for it not to be their fault. Knocking three times she almost jumped out of her skin when Tomeeka's dad answered the door.

Noticing that he'd startled her, he said, "Sorry to startle you Ashley, I was expecting a package and thought you were APS."

Covering up her uneasiness Ashley smiled and said as cheerily as she could muster, "It's ok, I'm just so used to Meeka or your wife answering the door."

"No problem, come on in, Tomeeka's upstairs", he said while stepping back to allow her to enter the foyer.

"Thanks", was all she said as she hurried to her friend's room. *Knock, knock, knock.* "Come in", called Tomeeka from the other side of the door.

"Oh Meeka, I think we made a big mistake", said Ashley on the verge of tears.

Taking one look at her friends face, Tomeeka jumped up and said, "What do you mean, what's wrong Ashley."

"Meeka, Tommy attacked Willie today at practice, and Willie is at County General right this minute. Coach even kicked Tommy off the team. Willie is hurt and hurt bad Meeka, and it's all our fault."

"Wait a minute, slow down Ashley. What happened, and from the beginning this time if you don't mind", said Tomeeka.

Sitting on the end of the bed and trying to calm her racing heart, Ashley took a deep breath and started from the beginning.

"I just saw Felicia, who said that Mitchell told her that Tommy attacked Big Willie at practice today. She then said that Willie couldn't get up, so doc examined him and then as they took him off the field he collapsed and had to go to County General. Next she said that Coach yelled at Tommy for an explanation, and when he didn't get one, threw him off the team."

"So what does that have to do with us", asked Tomeeka.

"Meeka, think..., we put that phony secret admirer note in Angie's locker", answered Ashley,

"And, what does that have to do with..., Oh my God, you don't think that Angie told Tommy it was from Willie do you", exclaimed a now upset Tomeeka.

"Meeka, girl, I'm not sure what happened, but I got a bad feeling about this", muttered Ashley while wringing her hands.

Gathering her purse and keys, Tomeeka said, "Come on, we got to get to the hospital and check on Willie." The two friends left without wasting a moment of precious time. Each hoping a praying that their actions had not caused their friend to be injured.

Chapter Fourteen

The hospital nursing staff was overwhelmed with the presence of all the concerned students that had shown up to inquire about their fellow classmate. Looking at the security guards, the head nurse said, "Something must be done about all these kids."

"What would you like for us to do, they're not causing any trouble", asked the officer.

"Let them know that only his immediate family is allowed to visit, and that they need to clear the waiting room for others visiting with their sick family members", she snapped.

Watching her walk back towards the ward, he shook his head and then moved to do as she asked. Raising his hands he made sure to have everyone's attention before saying, "Listen, I know that everyone is concerned about the young man from Lakeside High, but I am going to have to ask that you all go home and wait for an update from school officials."

"But Sir, we're not doing anything wrong, we just waitin for a chance ta see our friend", answered Mitchell.

"Hospital rules are that only the family is allowed to visit while the patient is in the Emergency room. I'm sorry but you all will have to wait until he moves into a permanent room", the security officer informed them.

Standing Ashley said quickly, "Well can you at least tell us how he's doing."

"I'm sorry young lady but I can't release any information on the patient's condition without the consent of his family, now you'll all have to go now", he said while ushering them outside.

The group of about 20 students walked slowly out of the ER and out into the parking lot. Some left on foot, while others drove away in their cars with concern marring their young features. Tomeeka and Ashley drove towards their neighborhood each lost in her own thoughts. Finally pulling up to her house, Tomeeka turned to Ashley and said, "I think it's time we told Angie what we did."

"How'd I know you were going to say that", asked Ashley with a look of pure dread reflected in her eyes.

Both girls exited the car and made their way to the Hill's front door. Ashley fidgeted while Tomeeka patted her foot nervously until the door opened. Angie took one look at their faces and knew that something big was going on. "Let's go upstairs", she said as she turned and made for the stairs. "Mom, it's Ashley, and Tomeeka, we'll be upstairs", she called out when they were halfway upstairs.

"Ok dear, let me know if you guys need anything", came the reply from her mother.

After closing the bedroom door she turned and asked, "What is it, what's going on."

Swallowing past the lump in her throat Tomeeka tried to find the right words to tell her friend what they'd done. "Today, I mean this afternoon, we,uh…"

A Woman of Honor; A Child of God

"We wrote you that stupid note and now Willie's in the hospital because of it", blurted Ashley.

"What", asked a confused Angie.

"Can we sit down Angie", asked Tomeeka while trying to gather the nerve to tell her friend what was going on.

"Oh, yeah, my bad, sit down", said Angie.

"This afternoon, we, Ashley, and myself, wrote that stupid love note, signed it secret admirer and then put it in your locker."

Laughing Angie, said, "Is that all that's got you two so dire faced."

"No Angie there's more", said Ashley.

Turning to face her friend who sounded as if she would break down in tears at any moment, Angie asked, "What are you trying not to tell me, Meeka, and what does it have to do with Big Willie."

"Angie, we're almost sure that Tommy somehow thinks it was Willie who sent you the note", answered Tomeeka.

"What, do you know what Tommy will do to Willie, please tell me you didn't let it slip that the note came from Willie", Angie demanded excitedly.

"No, we didn't tell anyone and that's why we don't understand what happened between Willie and Tommy", cried Ashley.

"What do you mean, what happened between Tommy, and Willie", said Angie as she came up off the chair.

"Uh… Angie, Tommy attacked Willie during football practice, Willie ended up in the hospital, and Tommy's off the team", Tomeeka said as she closed her eyes and waited for the explosion she knew was just a second away.

"Off the team, Tommy's off the team, because he attacked Willie, and it's all because of you two", exclaimed Angie.

"Angie listen, we didn't mean for any of this to happen. We didn't even know that Tommy would find out about the note, we thought you'd keep it to yourself", Ashley tried to explain haphazardly.

"Oh, no you're not going to try an blame me for any of this. This whole big mess is your fault", she said while pointing at the two of them.

"You're right Angie it's all our fault, we're so sorry", answered Tomeeka.

"Off the team, aw man, Tommy must be reeling", came the reply from Angie.

"Tommy", yelled Ashley. "Girl Willie is lying in a hospital bed, in who knows what condition, and you're worried about Tommy."

"Yes I'm worried about Tommy, and Willie is in a hospital bed because of you two, not Tommy", charged Angie.

Unable to comprehend the turn of this conversation, Tomeeka said, "Wait a minute Tommy is the one who attacked Willie, he's the reason Willie's in the ER, Angie."

"No Willie's in the ER because you two couldn't mind your own business, once again", shot back Angie hotly.

"Angie, Tomeeka, stop it now. Willie is in the hospital in who knows what condition; the why or the how doesn't matter. Guys Willie didn't deserve this, he didn't do anything wrong", stressed Ashley, hoping to squash the current argument.

"Ashley's right, Meeka, Willie and his condition is what really matters", replied a contrite Angie.

"Yeah, I agree, hey Angie do you think your parents could go with us down to the hospital, or maybe your Pastor could say a prayer or something", asked Tomeeka.

"It's worth a try, come on lets go", said Angie as she led her friends downstairs to talk to her parents.

Chapter Fifteen

The Principal came over the loud speaker promptly after the homeroom bell rang. *"Good Morning Students. As many of you know one of our fine young athletes was injured yesterday at practice. His condition is stable this morning, and he will be released sometime this week. He was found to have only a slight concussion, thankfully nothing too serious which could have been potentially dangerous for the young man. Now to the heart of the matter, this student was injured by another of our players, apparently there was some sort of issue that was unsettled between the two young men. I want all of you to hear me well this morning; this sort of behavior will not be tolerated at Lakeside High. As a result of the incident, Mr. Thomas Ellison, has been expelled from the team, as well as this school for the remainder of this school year."* Gasps were heard all around the school at this last statement. *"No one, I repeat, no one, physically harms another student because of differences of opinions. We here at Lakeside High will continue to strive for academic excellence, and will continue to display sportsmanship while on the athletic fields and arenas. I urge each of you to learn from this incident, and to take this lesson learned with you for the rest of your lives. Differences of opinions, and disagreements can be settled in a civilized manner, without doing injury to one another. Good Day, Students."*

Angie felt as if the wind had been knocked out of her. Try as she might, she couldn't seem to catch her breath. Noticing what was happening one of her classmates called out to the teacher saying, "Ms. Wallace, Angie's sick."

Rushing over to check on the young lady, Ms. Wallace sent one of the students to hit the intercom button and call for the school nurse.

"Angie, Ms. Hill, can you tell me what's wrong", asked Ms. Wallace.

"Yeah, her man been expelled", someone said cruelly. The others snickered as this announcement was made, which seemed to further distress Angie.

"Everyone sit down and keep your mouths closed", ordered Ms. Wallace.

Ashley made her way to Angie, and spoke calming words into her ear. Whispering she said, "Come on girlfriend get control, don't give these jerks nothing to talk about, breathe deeply Angie." Noticing that her friend seemed to be responding, Angie whispered again, "Breathe Angie, yeah that's a girl, breathe slow and deep."

Ms. Wallace visibly breathed a sigh of relief that the Landry girl had seemed to know what to do, and wondered what was taking the nurse so long. "Alex Jacobs, go and see what is taking the nurse so long to get here."

"Yes ma'am", came the reply as he hurried down the corridor.

Finally the school nurse arrived with the Vice-Principal in tow. Making their way towards Angie the nurse pulls out her stethoscope and listens for a heartbeat. After not hearing any irregularities she asks, "Ms. Hill, how are you feeling."

Softly, Angie spoke up and said, "I'm okay, ma'am."

"Can you tell me what happened, do you have a history of asthma", asked the nurse.

"No ma'am, no asthma, I was just having trouble catching my breath for a moment, but I'm fine now, honest", Angie added for good measure.

Moving closer to ask a few questions of her own, the Vice Principal said, "Have you ever had panic attacks before?"

"Panic attacks? I've never had one of those", replied Angie.

"Well sometimes they can be brought on when a person is overly stressed", explained the nurse.

"Is that what I had, a panic attack", asked Angie.

"I think it is fair to say yes", supplied Vice Principal Hollis. "Is there anything going on that you'd like to talk about", she added.

"No ma'am", answered Angie, her mind falling and lighting on a thousand thoughts at once. Oh God, Tommy had been kicked out of school, Willie was in a hospital, and she was somehow part to blame. What to do, whom to tell, could she tell anyone? No she decided, she couldn't tell anyone without her friends being dragged into the spotlight and possibly getting expelled for their part in what had transpired.

Pulled out of her reverie, she heard the Mrs. Hollis comment, "Are you sure, that _no_ was a little shaky."

Sitting taller in her seat, Angie said more firmly this time, "Yes ma'am I'm sure."

Sighing loudly, Vice Principal Hollis said finally, "Well then, since there's nothing you'd like to discuss, do you feel able to return your studies?

"Yes ma'am, I'm feeling lots better now", replied Angie.

"Fine then, we will simply note that you were feeling unwell, but recovered. We will send the notification by mail to your parents", stated Mrs. Hollis while watching Angie closely.

Knowing that they were watching to see if this would affect her, Angie schooled her reaction and said simply, "Ok, and thanks for your concern, Mrs. Hollis."

Shaking her head, Mrs. Hollis turned to leave, but not before saying once more, "Ok, but if you'd like to talk about anything, go to see the counselor, she's there to listen."

After they left Angie felt as if she'd like to crawl under her desk and stay there. Everyone's eyes were all on her. She was sure that while some were truly concerned, others were secretly laughing at her. She felt her face flush with shame and embarrassment, and was grateful when Ms. Wallace said, "Alright, show's over let's return to our studies."

Angie heard her peers groan, and let out a breath of relief when Ms. Wallace picked up where she'd left off in the lesson plan.

Getting off the bus Angie headed down the block; but was ill prepared for what happened next. Just as she rounded the corner and headed towards her house, two of her classmates stood talking to a young lady, who was holding a baby. Angie recognized her as the young lady she'd seen one night waiting outside the field house. She stiffened as she heard one of the girls say, "Dats hur, girlfriend, da one Tommy been sneaking round wit."

Stopping a few feet away she asked, "What did you say about Tommy and I."

"I said, you da one he been creepin with, behind Monique's back", replied the one Angie knew as A'quanetta.

"What do you mean creepin, Tommy and I have been dating since the beginning of the school year", Angie informed them.

"You don't say", responded the one she figured must be Monique. Sizing Angie up she went on to say, "We been together goin on three years, got a son to prove it, and another on the way fa dat matter."

"No, what you're saying can't possibly be true. Besides Tommy told me it was over between you two", Angie said with despair threatening to choke her.

She felt the bile rising as Monique said smugly, "Girl you weren't nuthin but a passin grade for Tommy. He needed ta stay on da team, so he could make a good life fa us, me, him and da babies."

Angie felt as if the wind had been knocked out of her. Her heart was wrenching in two. Unwilling to let one tear fall, she stepped around them and ran for her house. Knowing she was on the verge of a genuine melt down, she dashed through the front door, and upstairs to her room before her mother could even get a glimpse of her. She knew without a doubt that if her mother suspected in any way at all that there was something wrong, she would not rest until she knew all the details. Angie just simply wasn't up to being probed right now. Entering her bathroom and turning on the shower, she stripped and stood under the steady stream, letting her tears blend with the water flowing over her head. Finally when she'd exhausted all her tears, she shut off the shower and stepped out onto the rug. Reaching for a towel she dried herself off, and moved to find her favorite pair of sweats. After dressing in her old faded sweats and putting a pair of warm fuzzy socks on, she crawled into bed, and curled into a ball.

"Why, Tommy, why did you do this to me", she asked in the quietness of her bedroom, before allowing the lone tear to run down her cheek onto her pillow.

Chapter Sixteen

Angie Knew that she couldn't hide out any longer. It had been two hours since she'd come home and gone straight upstairs. Of a certainty she knew her mother would knock softly any moment. Going to the mirror she scrutinized her face for any tell tale signs of the misery she was going through. Satisfied that all seemed to be in order, she straightened her shoulders and walked towards the door, while saying, "Life goes on Angie girl, chalk this up as one of life's lessons."

Her mother looked up when she entered the room. Pasting as cheerful a smile as she could muster, Angie said, "Hi, Mom, sorry I've been locked up there so long, but I had a very important paper to finish."

"I understand sweetheart, besides you've gotta keep your grades up if you're going to get that scholarship", her mother quipped while folding towels.

"Need any help with those", Angie asked, indicating the towels and sheets her mother was busy folding.

"No, I can handle a little laundry, why don't you go over to Tomeeka's before your dad comes home."

Giving off a small laugh Angie says, "Yeah you're right, he does love for us all to sit and eat together." Looking back before stepping through the door she added, "I won't be long Mom."

Tomeeka took one look at Angie and knew that she'd been crying her heart out. Ushering her upstairs, she closed the door, pointed towards the bed, picked up the receiver and called Ashley.

"Ash, it's me Meeka, can you come over." "Ok". "We'll be waiting."

Angie was grateful that Tomeeka didn't try to push her for details while they were waiting for Ashley to arrive. Over and over again she heard Monique say that she and Tommy were expecting another child. How could Tommy lie to her this way? Had everything he said over these last months, been lies? Angie closed her eyes for a moment and wished again for the hundredth time she could make the thoughts swirling in her brain's depths disappear, cease to exist.

She was so lost in her misery that she didn't even notice Tomeeka opening the door for Ashley. When she finally came back to reality, it was to find both of her friends staring intently into her face with a look of pure disdain upon their faces.

"Angie, did you just hear anything I said, at all", asked Ashley.

Stammering over her response Angie said, "What, no I'm sorry, my mind was somewhere else."

"Ah girl, he's really hurt you this time hasn't he", asked Tomeeka.

Dropping her head into her hands Angie cried while nodding yes. Hugging their friend the girls both tried to reassure her by whispering words of encouragement.

"Don't worry, Angie everything will be ok." "Yeah, listen to Ashley", encouraged Tomeeka. "I know what it feels like to break up with somebody you love, but over time you'll be back to normal", Ashley told her friend.

A Woman of Honor; A Child of God

Two days later, Willie looked up as Angie, Ashley, and Tomeeka walked into his room. He smiled and greeted them cheerfully, "Hey what's up ladies."

Returning the greeting they each replied that he was the reason for their visit. Walking closer to the bed, Angie asked, "How are you feeling Willie."

"Ah, I'm fine, takes more than a bump on the head to do me in", he answered while shrugging his shoulders.

Moving forward Tomeeka let out a sigh of relief while saying, "Whew, are we glad to hear that, we've been so worried."

"Yes we have, we've all been worried sick", added Ashley.

"That's good to hear", Willie replied sheepishly. Turning his attention back to Angie, he asked, "How are you Angie."

Startled, Angie looked up and said, "Me, I'm fine, why do you ask."

"Just concerned about you, that's all", Willie said quickly. An embarrassing silence filled the room at that point. Angie turned to stare out of the window, while Willie darted a nervous glance towards Tomeeka and Ashley. Hoping to fill the silence and ease the tension in the room, Ashley began to tell Willie about all the recent events taking place in History class. In no time at all the normalcy returned as they all laughed and took part in the discussion.

Sooner than they thought, the nurse came over the P.A. system, announcing that visiting hours were over. Rising one by one they all said their goodbyes and wished Willie a good night.

"Goodnight Willie, we'll come back soon", Angie said as she walked towards the door.

"Ok, thanks again for dropping by", Willie said softly.

Casting one more glance towards the hospital bed Angie smiled and waved goodbye. Pulling in the door she looked up to find her two best friends staring at her expectantly.

Pulling up short she asked, "What."

"Nothing", replied Ashley and glanced towards Tomeeka before turning and walking away.

Convinced that they were up to something, Angie stopped just short of the elevators and demanded to know what they were cooking up. "I know that the wheels are spinning, so fess up you two."

Placing her hand on Angie's shoulder, Ashley asked incredulously, "You have no idea do you."

"What are you talking about Ash, did I do something wrong back there", Angie asked as she inclined her head towards Willie's room.

"No, you didn't do anything wrong at all. You did everything right for a change", answered Tomeeka.

Blowing out a sigh of exasperation, Ashley stepped into the open elevator and beckoned to her friends. "Come on, we'll explain it all in the car."

Angie listened in stunned silence as her friends went over what they believed to be the obvious. She found herself shaking her head no, and realized that her mouth had dropped open and seemed to be stuck in this position. She couldn't possibly bring herself to believe what they were saying.

"Guys, surely you are letting your imaginations run wild. Willie isn't interested in me", denied Angie.

"Girl, It hurt me to see the disappointment on his face when he realized that you had no idea how he felt for you", Ashley pointed out.

"Angie, didn't you notice his concern for you", asked Tomeeka.

"All he did was ask how I was, what's the big deal. Don't read anything into this guys, please", pleaded Angie.

Looking at one another the girls decided to leave things as they were. Reaching over Ashley put in a new CD and adjusted the volume. Soon they were all engaged in singing the popular tune, as each girl lost herself to the beat of the soul stirring music. Dropping off Ashley, Tomeeka and Angie said their goodbyes. Hopping into the front seat, Angie waved one last time and buckled up as Tomeeka pulled away from the curb.

Reaching their destination both girls got out of the car and said their goodnights. Tomeeka stood on the porch until Angie reached the front door. Just as she was about to go inside Angie heard Tomeeka say, "See ya tomorrow, my girl."

Sticking her head back out of the door, Angie said in a voice filled with mirth, "Ok, goodnight and thanks."

That night she said a little extra prayer for Willie and thanked God for healing him, and making everything alright.

Chapter Seventeen

Lakeside High was abuzz with conversation, over Willie's return to school. It had been a whole week since the day of the incident involving the two football players, and everyone had their own opinion over what had transpired. Those who supported Willie agreed with the Principal's decision to expel Tommy for the remainder of the school year. Those who were on Tommy's side objected and thought the punishment too harsh for what had transpired between the two rivals. On the day of Willie's return, the gap between to the two factions of students still had not been bridged.

Angie and the others listened as once again the Principal came over the P.A. system to give a brief synopsis and to welcome Willie back to the school's campus. As soon as the announcements were over, Ms. Davis promptly began with the day's lesson plan. Several times during the lecture, Angie looked up to find Willie watching her, however he looked away each time their eyes met. Confounded at this new behavior from Willie, Angie found herself fidgeting through the remainder of class.

As soon as the bell rung, she made her way out of class and towards her next subject. Tomeeka had to run to catch up with her, calling to her friend she cried out, "Hey, Angie, wait up."

Turning to face her friend Angie apologized. "I'm sorry Meeka, I'm just anxious to get to class that's all."

"What", Tomeeka asked with a look of utter disbelief. "You're anxious to get to Ms. Wolfe's class", she asked skeptically. Everyone knew that Ms. Wolfe's lectures put the "o" in the word boring.

Realizing what she'd just said, Angie laughed and said, "What am I saying."

"I think you were trying to convince me as well as yourself that you actually enjoy American History class", Angie replied with a smirk.

"Meeka, something's going on", Angie said with a confounded look marring her face.

Concern now leaping to life, Tomeeka asked urgently, "What do mean, what happened."

Wringing her hands Angie mulled over what she should say, and how to say it. Several times over the last hour she'd felt her spine tinkling as she looked up and found Willie watching her. She had never seen Willie look at her this way before, why now for God's sake? I mean her emotions were all in turmoil. She wasn't even sure of what she thought she'd seen. Was she simply imagining things or had Willie really been looking at her differently?

"Well are you going to tell me what has you so up in arms", asked Tomeeka.

"Nothing really, let me think on things some more, I'm not even sure of what I saw", Angie said absently.

"Tell me, Angie, whatever it is, is seems to have you puzzled", urged her friend.

Just as she was about to share her concerns with Meeka, Willie walked up and asked Angie if he could speak with her for a moment. "Angie can I have a minute of your time?"

Tied-tongued Angie managed to say, "I guess so."

A Woman of Honor; A Child of God

Taking Angie by the elbow he lead her towards her next class, Willie took a deep breath before saying, "Angie I, …I… I'd like to…"

"You'd like to what, Willie", she interrupted nervously.

"I,…I mean, what I'm trying to say, is", was all he managed before losing his nerve. Dropping his hand from her elbow, he backed away, and said sadly, "Nothing, I'm sorry I bothered you."

More puzzled than ever, Angie watched as he walked away. She stepped inside the class just as the tardy bell sounded. Taking her seat she glanced in Tomeeka's direction and shook her head no, while humping her shoulders, to indicate that she had no idea what had been on Willie's mind.

Willie sat in Trigonometry lost to his own tangled thoughts. He felt like kicking himself over his recent disastrous attempt at a discussion with Angie. Surely at this very moment, Angie must be calling him every kind of fool she could think of. How could he have been so stupid? What had convinced him to try and talk to her, tell her of his feelings? Not even he was sure of what he really felt for her. On one hand he knew that he cared for her, but how deeply? Were his feelings for her genuine or was it just infatuation with whom she seemed to be? Looking down at his paper, he turned his attention to his given assignment and systematically worked out the problems.

Angie found herself doodling instead of paying attention to the lecture on the War of 1812. Looking at her notes, she nearly gasped aloud as she realized, she had been forming a "W", in the sidelines of her paper. What in the world was going on now? Shaking her head to clear it, she tried to focus on the lecture but found her thoughts drifting to Willie again. What had he been trying to say? Why was she feeling all warm inside when he was around? Were Tomeeka and Angie wearing her down with their talk of Willie having feelings for her? She decided on the latter, that had to be it. All their talk about Willie caring for her was causing her to somehow think that she also had feelings for him. Yeah that was it; I mean hey she still loved Tommy, didn't she? Somehow, though try as she might, she couldn't conjure up all those feelings of love for Tommy like she used to.

Chapter Eighteen

The Youth/Young Adult Choir marched in singing, "Praises unto God on High", that 2nd Sunday. As usual the second Sunday of every month was Youth/ Young Adult Sunday. The service was conducted by the Young People; even the sermon was brought by the Youth Pastor. Angie was astonished as Willie took the microphone and sang the lead. The normal lead hadn't shown up for Church and the Minister of Music had called for a substitute. She had been shocked to find out that Willie could sing. Why had she never noticed this before, sure she'd known him since childhood, due to the fact they'd grown up in Christian House of Praise Worship Center, but singing like this? She was so shocked by the sound of his anointed voice that she almost missed the cue for the altos to come in on the refrain.

All during service she caught herself glancing his way. A couple of times when she'd looked up, she had found him looking at her strangely. Thinking that he was probably wondering why she kept looking at him, she willed her eyes to stare down at the passage of scripture the Youth Pastor was expounding upon. Soon she was caught up in the sermon with the rest of the congregation, and found herself witnessing the young man as he began the close of his sermon. *"Oh Hallelujah, one of these old days, I will be called up, you shall be called up, all of God's Children shall be called up. We're going to a place where there is no sorrow, no trials and tribulations, no sickness, no distress. They tell me that the street is paved with gold there, Ohhhh, I don't believe you heard me this morning. I said I'm going to be called up to take residence in the mansion He has prepared for me. Soon I will be done with the troubles and the cares of this world. Hallelujah, by and by, what a day of rejoicing there shall be when all God's children get to Heaven; do I have a witness this morning? I tell you He died on and old rugged cross, one Friday evening, but early that Sunday morning, He got up. I said He got up, with power, all power in His hands. Power to save me, power to raise me, power to draw me nearer. I tell you He got up and because He got up, I too shall get up, you're gonna get up, all mankind shall get up. Saved and unsaved shall get up, and stand before him on that great getting up morning. I praise Him for getting up; he defeated death when he rose. No grave can hold me, because He got up, do I have witness this morning? Oh death where is thy sting, grave where is thy victory? I shall rise when the trumpet sounds. I shall rise above the rooftops, I shall rise above the treetops, I shall rise above the clouds, I shall rise above the moon, sun and stars. I tell you I shall rise, till I reach Heaven. Do I have a witness this morning? Praise be unto God, the Lord of Lords, the King of Kings, I'm going to get up again and ascend into Heaven. I knowwwwwwwwwwww I shall rise again, Do you know that you shall get up again? If you know that you know, that you know, that you know, you're going to rise again, you ought to stand to your feet, and shout, Hallelujah, Praise be unto the Most High God. Don't fool me now, If you know that when the trumpet sounds, that you shall get up out of that grave, shout, shout, shout, I said shout. Hallelujah, yeahhhhhhhhhh, yeah, yeah. I shall riseeeeeeeeeee again."*

Angie watched as he concluded and opened the doors of the Church. She rejoiced with everyone else as five new people came forward to give their lives to Christ. Three of them were awaiting candidates of Baptism.

A Woman of Honor; A Child of God

After the conclusion of the services Angie exited the choir stand, and moved to find her parents. She came to a halt when she saw that they were talking with Willie's parents. She felt her heart beat quicken as her father motioned her over.

Oh God this couldn't be happening. What could her Parent's possibly be doing speaking with the Dillard's? Forcing one foot in front of the other, she made her way slowly to her Father's side and greeted everyone. "Hi, Mom, Dad, Mr. And Mrs. Dillard, did you all enjoy the service? "Oh yes,, God truly moved in this place", answered Willie's mom.

"Yes he did, do that", agreed Mrs. Hill. "Angie we were just speaking with the Dillard's about going out to eat with us this afternoon", her mother explained.

"Yes, and we were looking around to see if we could find you and William", her father added.

"There he is, Willie, over here", his mother called out.

He groaned inwardly when he spied his parents standing there with Angie and her parents. Forcing a small to his face, he said as cheerfully as he could muster, "Hello, everyone."

"Hello young man, that was some fine singing you did today", Mrs. Hill stated. "Yes some fine singing indeed", echoed Mr. Hill.

Feeling uncomfortable, Willie thanked them for their compliments shyly and wished only to be as far away from Angie as possible. "Thanks and praise God that I was able to fill in. Well, I guess we'd better get going", he suggested to his parent's hopefully.

"Good idea, my stomach is growling unbearably at this very moment", chimed in his father. Smiling he turned to say goodbye to Angie, but instead nearly swallowed his tongue when he heard his father ask his mother and Mrs. Hill if they had a place in mind. "Do you ladies have a place in mind for lunch."

"We're going to lunch with the Hill's", Willie asked a little too loudly. Both sets of parents laughed and shook their heads that yes, they were all going to lunch together. He fell silent and glanced in Angie's direction. He noticed that she was just as ill at ease as he was, and so as not to cause her anymore discomfort, he kept quiet, and moved to follow them out of the church.

On the way to the restaurant, Angie's mind wandered aimlessly over what had been uppermost in her mind for the last three weeks. She let out a sigh and thanked God that there were only three more weeks of school left, and then she would graduate and go on to college. Please Lord she prayed, let these weeks go by quickly.

Noticing that her mind seemed to be elsewhere, her father hunched her mother and indicated the back seat. Looking through her vanity mirror, her mother smiled knowingly and winked at her husband. It seemed her husband had been right again, in suggesting that their daughter and the Dillard boy had feelings for each other. Just yesterday he'd said, *"Honey, I'm willing to bet that they care for one another, but just don't know what to do about it."*

How in the world had he known such a thing? She had to admit, her husband was some kind of man.

In the car behind them, Mr. And Mrs. Dillard shared a conspiratorial wink, as they both remembered the conversation, they'd shared the day before about William and Angela. They couldn't have been happier about what had been transpiring between these two over the last several weeks.

"William, you seem awfully quiet, is anything wrong", asked his mother.

"Naw, Mom everything's fine", he answered while falling silent once again, and losing himself to his thoughts. These last few weeks had been nothing but a mumble jumble of feelings

A Woman of Honor; A Child of God

and thoughts of Angie. Not only was his mind always on her, she was even showing up in his dreams.

"You did a marvelous job today Son", his father stated proudly.

"Thanks dad", Willie answered and then fell silent again.

Reaching the all you can eat buffet, both sets of parent's entered and were followed by their absent minded children. Filling her plate Angie returned to the table and was shocked to find her plate full of heart shaped cookies.

Laughing her father said playfully, "Sweetheart, don't you think that it would be better to eat some solid food first, and then dessert."

"I just wanted to make sure that there would be some left, you know how fast those things disappear." Grabbing up a plate she made a dash for the buffet once again, and this time tried to keep her mind focused on choosing her meal. Satisfied that she had an acceptable meal on her plate, she headed for the table. She nearly stumbled when she saw that the only open seat was the one next to Willie's.

Her father had to cough into his napkin, to keep from letting the laughter inside ripple freely. The look on his daughter's face had been priceless. Her mother reached under the table and poked him, reminding him to keep a civil tongue in his head. She was sure that Angie would never forgive him if he embarrassed her in anyway. They all ate in unbearable silence. I mean the silence was so thick; you could have cut it with a butter knife.

Trying to lighten the atmosphere Angie heard Mr. Dillard ask her about her plans after graduation. "Well, have you decided on a College yet Angela"?

"Uh, Yes sir, I'll be attending Mc Neal State University", she replied but couldn't finish because Willie had gone into a fit of coughing. His mother whacked him on the back and offered him some water. Mr. Dillard however was enjoying this too much, and explained what was happening, "William just accepted a scholarship from them as well, huh what do you know, you two will be seeing a lot more of each other."

Angie's appetite was suddenly gone; she placed her fork down and tried to steady her breathing. Noticing her discomfort, her mother spoke up and came to her rescue. "Sweetheart, would you mind terribly getting me another soft drink"?

Seizing the opportunity, Angie left the table and went to refill her mother's glass. Finally able to control his fit of coughing, Willie gulped a breath of fresh air, and offered and apology, "Guess it just went down the wrong way."

"Yes, that certainly happens from time to time", beamed Mr. Hill. Mrs. Hill could have kicked him; he looked so pleased with himself. She could have sworn that she saw He and Mr. Dillard wink at each other across the table, conspicuously.

Angie once again took her seat, and waited for the questions to begin anew. She didn't have long to wait. Just as she placed a cookie up to her mouth, she heard her father ask Willie, "So William, what made you choose Mc Neal U?"

"I, uh, I mean, they offered me a great scholarship, and I don't have to move far away. I can come home every weekend, and make the, "Young Adult Group Meetings", on Saturday evenings", he replied.

"And you Angela, why did you choose Mc Neal", asked Mr. Dillard.

"Same reasons", Angie said without elaborating.

To cover the awkward silence, Mrs. Hill said to no one in particular, "Aren't these yeast rolls wonderful."

"Yes, they certainly are", chimed in Mrs. Dillard, while shooting a warning glance at her husband. Her eyes promised a tongue lashing out of this world if he didn't stop putting these two young people on the hot burner.

"Yes well it is a good choice nevertheless. In fact I graduated from Mc Neal, as well as you own Father", noted Mr. Dillard.

"Yes sir", was the only reply she gave.

"I'm sure you two will find Mc Neal as wonderful an experience as we found it", stated Mr. Hill.

"Say I have a wonderful idea, Prom is next week, are you two considering attending", Mr. Hill pressed onward. His wife nearly screeched aloud at his audacity. This time she did indeed kick him under the table.

Angie looked as if she might die of the embarrassment, while Willie looked as if he would expire at any moment.

"Uh, no sir, I don't think I'll be attending this year's prom", Willie answered.

"What you won't be attending, but why", Angie suddenly turned and asked to her father's utter delight.

"I'm just not interested in going that's all", Willie, said with a shrug.

"But Willie, you're sure to be crowned King, I mean everybody's talking about it", pressed Angie.

"Really, they're talking about voting me for King", asked a now interested Willie.

"Yes, really, that's all the cheering squads having been discussing for the last month. In fact they're the ones behind your nomination", Angie informed him.

"Ah that's krump, Me, King of Prom", exclaimed Willie.

"Yeah, it would be a real let down if you didn't attend, they're really hyped about this, Willie", Angie informed him.

Chapter Nineteen

Looking on Mr. Hill and Mr. Dillard beamed with their success. While their mothers looked on with hopeful expectancy.

The two teens were suddenly lost in their conversation about the upcoming Prom and Graduation. In the back of Angie's mind she took note of the fact that they were both speaking to each other with ease. Gone was the nervousness. She looked down at her hands and noticed that they were no longer sweating in fact her hand was resting comfortably on his forearm. Snatching it away quickly before he noticed she placed her hand back on her lap.

Where her hand had been however, did not go unnoticed by Willie. The fact was he could still feel her hand resting there even though it was now firmly in her lap. If he concentrated real hard he could still feel the warmth left by the imprint of her hand. Encouraged by the ease with which they were communicating, Willie took a leap of faith. Looking into her eyes, he asked gently, "Angie will you go to Prom with me, I mean that's if you don't already have a date"?

"I accept, I'll be delighted to be your date", Angie answered feeling as though a thousand pound weight had now been lifted from her shoulders. She couldn't fathom this new feeling, the constriction that had bound her heart for the last several months was gone.

Mr. Hill couldn't contain himself any longer, and interrupted the teens. "Well aren't you two glad we had lunch today." Turning to his wife, he said with a smile, "Looks like you two will be doing some shopping this week."

Chuckling Mrs. Hill replied, "You are just too much. Don't pay him any attention Angie, you know how he loves to tease."

"Well son, looks like we've got to get you fitted for your tux", Mr. Dillard added quickly.

"Guess so dad", Willie replied simply.

Placing her napkin on the table Mrs. Dillard looked towards the Hill's and said, "Thank You all for a lovely afternoon, I'm so glad we spent this time fellowshipping together."

Following her lead, everyone else returned their napkins to the table and stood to take their leave. Willie helped Angie pull out her chair and smiled briefly as their eyes met.

"Thanks", she said shyly. Moving to stand next to her parents she glanced once more at Willie, and was struck by just how handsome he was. Wow, she'd never really noticed that he had light cocoa brown eyes and dimples. Willie had dimples, how could she have missed that?

Running upstairs to change her clothes quickly, Angie selected a pair of jeans and a t-shirt. Grabbing a pair of socks and her sneakers she made her way back down the stairs and said excitedly, "Mom, Dad, I'll be over at Meeka's."

"Ok sweetpea", came her Mother's reply.

Unable to refrain from gloating another minute Mr. Hill said to Mrs. Hill, "Tell me I don't know what's going on." "Didn't I tell you there were sparks flying between those two."?

"Yes you told me", Mrs. Hill answered.

"Uh uh, that's not good enough. Say it, come on, say it", he urged with all the glee of a four year old opening a birthday present.

"Alright, you were right and I was wrong", admitted Mrs. Hill to his utmost satisfaction.

"I know I am, I'm always right", he added with enough arrogance to choke and elephant.

Laughing she said, "Now, I wouldn't go that far."

"Well maybe not always, but most of the time, you've got to admit though, I'm usually right on the mark", Mr. Hill responded.

"Ok, I'll agree to usually, but no way am I going to agree with always", she answered with another chuckle.

Spreading his hands he asked, "Well since we have all this time on our hands, want to catch a Matinee."

"Sure, why not", she asked as they made their way downstairs to the family room.

While her husband made his over to the television and searched for a Sunday Matinee, Mrs. Hill went in search of popcorn and drinks. After all what was a good movie, without popcorn?

Chapter Twenty

Angie could hardly contain herself as she made her way upstairs to Tomeeka's room. Before knocking she could hear that Ashley, and Felicia were already here. Great now they wouldn't have to call them over and wait for them to arrive. *Knock, knock, knock.*

"Come in", came the call from Tomeeka.

Entered she greeted everyone cheerfully, "Hello everyone, am I ever glad you're all here."

Piqued they all turned to return the greeting. Tomeeka took one look at Angie's face and knew that something big had happened. The spark was back in her friend's eye. "*Oh God, she prayed, please don't let Tommy have anything to do with this change of behavior in Angie, please, please, please, please.*" After whispering this silent prayer she took a deep breath and said, "Sit down, and tell us everything, and I mean don't leave anything out."

Ashley sat up straighter and listened intently to what Angie was saying. Felicia however was too excited to stay quiet, and interrupted a couple of times, only to be shushed by the other two girls.

Standing with her hand in mid air, Tomeeka said in a dreamlike voice, "You and Willie are going to prom together."

With a whoop of laughter Ashley sprung to her feet and hugged Angie as if her very life depended upon that hug. Felicia clapped and shouted, "Yeah, yeah, yeah, that's what I'm talking bout."

Angie giggled and said, "Hey did you know that Willie has dimples"?

"Dimples", they all said in unison.

"Yes he has dimples, and light cocoa brown eyes", Angie informed them.

"Light cocoa brown eyes", Ashley asked with a hint of sarcasm, "Sure they're not mocha brown?

"Oh no, they're light cocoa brown", Angie answered without noticing the mirth threatening to spill forth from Ashley, Tomeeka, and Felicia.

"Just checkin, is all", Ashley said before they all burst into laughter.

"What's so funny, all I said was that he had dimples and light… *hahahaha*, Ok, ok, I see what's so funny", she said finally.

"So, what are you going to wear girlfriend", asked Felicia.

Bringing both hands up to her cheeks, Angie confessed, "I don't have a clue. You guys know that I wasn't even planning on going, I don't even know what color he's wearing."

"Don't sweat it girl, we'll take care of everything", announced Felicia.

Turning to face her Tomeeka asked, "We will, just how do we take care of everything"?

Grabbing up her handbag she said, "We hit the mall, today, right now. Let's go homeys."

Heading out of the door Angie said, "I need to get my bag and some money from Dad, meet me at the house." Rushing down the stairs she went inside and informed her parents they were heading to the mall, and asked for the cash.

"Meeka and the gang are going to help me find something for the prom, dad can I have some money, please", she said nonchalantly.

"But, I thought you and Mom were going to find a dress", her father asked.

"No, dear, I think it's fine that Angie and her friends will pick out the dress", her mother answered.

Hugging her Mom, Angie placed a small kiss on her cheek and said, "Thanks Mom, I knew you'd understand."

Pulling out his wallet, her father signed a blank draft, and told her, "Whatever you do young lady, don't lose this, someone could clear us out if you did."

Taking the check Angie chuckled and answered, "Don't worry Dad, I won't lose it." Kissing them both she placed the check in her wallet, grabbed her keys and hurried out to meet her friends.

Taking his wife into the circle of his arms, Mr. Hill said, "You're a superb Mom, did you know that."

"Superb, am I", she asked playfully.

"Yes, stupendous! I know that you had your heart set on going with our daughter to pick out her dress", he stated.

Snuggling deeper against his chest she replied, "Thank you honey, I really needed that."

"I know, I know", was all he said as he kissed the top of his wife's head and hugged her tighter to himself.

Chapter Twenty-one

"The limo's here sweetie", called Mr. Hill.

Standing quickly Angie said to her Mom, "Oh Mom, I'm so nervous, I don't know if I can do this."

Taking her daughters hands into her own, Mrs. Hill said calmly, "Angie there's nothing to it. Simply put one foot in front of the other. Walk down those stairs, get into that car, and go and enjoy yourself."

"Yes ma'am, thank you Mom, you always know how to calm my fears", Angie said as she kissed her mother's cheek, and headed for the door.

Mr. Hill took a deep breath and swallowed the visible lump that had formed in his throat, as Angie came down the stairs. Gliding down the stairs was his baby girl dressed in the palest shade of blue he'd ever seen. There were crystal beads strewn all over the gown from the bodice to the skirt. She wore diamonds in her ears, and around her neck. Her hair had been swept up into a French roll, and tiny rain curls cascaded down the left side of her face. She wore silver slippers on her feet, which matched her long gloves and small silver bag.

With his voice cracking he said softly, "Darling you're absolutely breathtaking."

Walking into his arms she said, "Oh Daddy, of course you'd think so."

"No baby, you look like a doll, a priceless porcelain doll", he said setting her away from him. Turning slightly he said, "If you don't believe me ask William." Stepping forward, Willie broke into a heart- wrenching smile at the vision before him. "Wow Angie you do that dress justice, I have to say that much."

"Thanks Willie, you working that Tux, yourself", replied Angie.

"Oh", said Willie, "Here's your corsage, it's one of the ones for your wrist."

Sticking out her wrist Angie basked in all the compliments and giggled as Willie and her Mother fastened the corsage to her silver gloves.

"Ready", Willie asked after the task had been completed.

"Yes, I am", Angie, said as she placed her hand at the bend in his arm. Looking back at her parents she wished them a good night and allowed Willie to seat her in the back of the limousine.

Mr. And Mrs. Hill waved goodbye until they turned the corner and were out of sight. Leaning back against the door, Mr. Hill said, "Thank God this is just her senior prom. I'm glad we have another four or five years before we watch her walk out that door to start her own family, I don't think my heart could stand it if it were any sooner."

Chuckling, Mrs. Hill held out her arms to him and said sympathetically, "Come on dear, you need a hug."

"Yes I do", replied her husband as he walked into her outstretched arms.

Angie and Willie rode chatting happily to the prom. Willie had her laughing and feeling as though she had not a care in the world. Angie couldn't believe she was having such a good time. Somehow she'd gotten the perception that Willie

A Woman of Honor; A Child of God

was boring, but she couldn't have dreamt of a more interesting, and exciting date.

Pulling up to the entrance, the driver got out of the car, walked to the back door, and opened it to allow Willie and Angie exit. Their friends were all waiting near the entrance and applauded as they entered the ballroom.

Hugging their friend, Ashley, Tomeeka, and Felicia, each told Angie how beautiful she was and teased her about her handsome date. "You're right, his eyes are light cocoa brown", whispered Tomeeka.

"And those dimples, girl, make a girl's heart do back flips", added Felicia saucily. To this pronouncement all the girls burst into another round of laughing. The guys fearing that they were the causes for such laughter cast furtive glances towards their dates. A. J. Stepped forward and said, "Hey, hey, hey, what's so funny."

Stepping next to him to rest her hand against his chest, Ashley said, "Don't worry, we weren't laughing at you."

"I hope it wasn't me", replied Mitchell. "Here, here, say it wasn't me", added Lance.

"No it wasn't you, or you, or you", answered Tomeeka as she turned to the other three young men. "We were just sharing an amusing observation", she went on to say.

"Alright, come on let's dance, you know that's my jam", stated Lance as he led Tomeeka to the dance floor. "Later guys", she called over her shoulder while being propelled towards the other dancers.

"Well, we might as well join in on all the fun", suggested Mitchell.

Clapping him on the shoulder, Willie held out his arm to Angie in invitation and said, "An excellent idea my man."

The couples headed towards the dance floor where they danced several rounds. When they just couldn't dance another step, they moved over to the refreshments table and got something to drink. Next they all took pictures, danced some more, got more refreshments and danced once more. Finally it was time to announce the King and Queen of Prom. The Vice-Principal took the stage and began to read off the nominations. Angie cheered along with everyone else as Willie's name was read off. The next nomination however left her speechless.

"Nominations for Prom Queen are, Angela Hill, Juanita Buckley, A'quanetta James, Nicole Jacobs, and Veronica Holmwood", announced the 1st Vice.

"Angie, Angie, Angie" the crowd cheered, which left no doubt in anyone's mind that she was this year's Queen.

Holding up her hands for silence The 1st Vice continued by saying, "This year's Prom King is Mr. William Dillard." The crowd went wild. The applause was thunderous to be exact. Angie congratulated him with a kiss on the cheek, and then he walked to the podium to receive his crown and robe. Quietening down the crowd again she said, "It gives me great pleasure to announce this year's Queen. Without further adieu, she is Ms. Angela Hill."

Rooted to the spot, Angie cried in disbelief, "Oh my God. No way, she didn't say me, did she."

Pushing her towards the stage, her friends kissed her cheeks, and assured her that yes she was this year's Queen.

As she reached the platform, Willie held out his hand and helped her up the steps. He watched with pride as the tiara was placed upon her head. He smiled at her as they draped the robe over her shoulders, and handed her the scepter.

Angie moved as if in a dream, and was grateful for Willie's strong hand at her elbow, and his clear head. She followed as he led her to the middle of the dance floor. Willie signaled the band and they played a waltz. She couldn't stop the tears from flowing as he swept her around and around the dance floor.

Looking down at her tear-streaked face he asked, "Are those tears of happiness, Angie or regret for it not being Tommy here with you tonight"?

Shaking her head vehemently she reassured him that her tears were tears of joy. "No, Willie, I don't regret anything about this night. I am just overjoyed at everything that's happened."

Looking into her eyes, he dipped his head and kissed her gently. So soft did his lips touch hers that for a moment she thought she was only imagining it. When he received no protest, Willie kissed her again.

Suddenly she was lost to a swirl of feelings. Time stood still for Angie, it seemed as if the ceiling had faded away and they were floating amongst the moon and stars. There was only Willie, and what he was making her feel. In the back of her mind, she wondered why she'd never felt anything like this when Tommy had kissed her? Shrugging the thought away, she snuggled closer and kissed him back, which sent electrical currents throughout his large framed body.

Only when the applause and catcalls from their friends penetrated their fogged brains, did they break the kiss. Embarrassed and afraid he'd done something wrong, Willie began to make an apology. "Angie, I'm sorry, I… didn't mean to…" he started by was cut off in mid sentence.

Looking directly into those beautiful eyes of his, Angie said, "Don't apologize Willie, just do it again please."

Smiling he said, "Nothing could please me more." Another round of cheering went up as they kissed again. Breaking off the kiss when the music stopped, Willie led Angie towards the photographer's booth to retrieve their pictures. Every thing from that point on seemed a blur as the night's events sped past her at the speed of light.

The evening wasn't long enough for Angie, not even after they all went to breakfast at the local Pancake house. She'd lost count of the number of times she and Willie had kissed. Even now they sat with their fingers intertwined.

Only a comment from Tomeeka drew her back to the present, "Girl, Angie, your parents are going to flip when they hear you were crowned Queen."

"Flip, my dad is going to lose his mind", Angie said to the laughter of everyone.

"Aw man, your pops is going to be off the hook, for the next week", added Willie.

"I know, I'll be lucky if he doesn't take out an ad in the newspaper to announce it to everyone in Lakeside", said a laughing Angie.

The waitress brought their meal and everyone lost themselves to the delicious taste of the restaurants famous pancakes and sausage.

Angie didn't want the evening to end and hated the thought of ending their magical night. As the limo pulled up outside of her home, she could have sworn she saw a lamp being turned off upstairs in her parent's room.

Walking her to the door, Willie said, "Thank you for the best evening I've ever had."

"I feel the same way Willie, thanks for escorting me tonight", Angie said shyly.

"Well, I guess I should be going now", suggested Willie.

"Ok, thanks again", replied Angie.

Inclining his head towards her, he placed another kiss on her lips. He then kissed her forehead, each cheek, her chin, and then finally her lips again. Just then the porch light blinked off and then on again. The two sprang apart, laughed and bid each other goodnight. Neither had any doubt, that it is Angie's dad on the other side of the front door.

Placing her key in the lock Angie entered the foyer to find her Father making a mad dash for the family room. Laughing she said goodnight to Willie and closed the door. "Give it up Dad, I already saw you", she said playfully.

A Woman of Honor; A Child of God

Coming around the corner Mr. Hill laughed and pulled Mrs. Hill to his side. Angie shook her head and laughed at the guilty looks on their faces.

"So, how did it go", her mother asked.

"Dear I think it's evident how things went, she and William seemed to be joined at the lips just a few moments ago", her Father stated frankly.

"Dad, we, we, we were only saying good night", protested Angie.

"Martin, behave yourself", came the reply from Mrs. Hill, to her daughter's relief.

"Well", she prompted, " Come on into the family room and tell us about your night."

"Queen", her parent's exclaimed in unison.

Giggling she said, "Yes Queen, I was selected Queen and Willie was selected King."

Clasping her hands to her chest, Mrs. Hill said through sheen of tears, "I'm so happy for you Angie." She then moved to hug her daughter. Her father, Mr. Hill, was however not so conventional with his response. "Yeah boy, queen, my baby girl queen. Hahahahaha, wait till the staff hears about this."

"Martin, calm down, and don't go rubbing Angie's selection for Queen in Mr. James' face either", she cautioned.

Looking the epitome of innocence, he said, "Me, rub it in his face, that Angie beat out A'quanetta, never."

Rolling her eyes heavenward Mrs. Hill said, "Oh brother we're in for it now."

"I know I shudder to think just how far he will go", Angie agreed. Standing Mrs. Hill stretched out her hand and said to her daughter, "Come on, lets turn in, he's going to bask in this for at least another hour, and it's already 3am."

Rising Angie followed her mother out of the room and upstairs towards her bedroom.

"Mom, can you help me out of this thing", she asked as they reached her door.

"Sure, do you want me to run you a bath", her mother inquired.

"Naw, I'll just take a shower", answered Angie.

"You young people and your showers. For us there was nothing better than an nice warm bubble bath", stated her Mother.

"A nice hot shower, will do the same thing, besides it takes less time to get ready", replied Angie with a smile.

Helping her daughter to get out of all the layers, Mrs. Hill said, "You looked so lovely tonight."

"Thanks Mom. I felt beautiful too", Angie confessed.

Chapter Twenty-two

Graduation came sooner than anyone realized. Mr. And Mrs. Hill beamed with their pride over Angie's accomplishments. She was Class Valedictorian and they couldn't have been more proud of her. Her father glanced over at the Dillard's and they looked just as proud of William.

"Those kids of ours are something special heh, Hill", asked Mr. Dillard.

"That they are friend, that they are", agreed Mr. Hill.

"Shush, you two the program is starting", whispered Mrs. Dillard. Their two husbands simply smiled and turned their attention to the opening of the ceremony. Willie looked back to catch a glimpse of Angie as her row stood to make their way towards the platform. As if on cue, Angie looked at him and smiled as he winked at her. Angie made her way unto the platform, received her mock diploma, posed for her picture, and then exited the stage. She returned to her seat as row by row stood and headed for the stage. Finally, when everyone had gotten their Diploma's the Principal proclaimed them all graduates.

A yell went up from the students as they hugged one another, and threw their caps into the air. Willie made his way towards Angie, lifted her feet from the ground and kissed her soundly in front of everyone, including their parents.

Clearing his throat Mr. Hill asked jokingly, "Mind if I hug my daughter now, Mr. William"

Stepping back, William smiled and said, "Not at all Mr. Hill, not at all." Turning he hugged his own parents, as well as Mrs. Hill. Soon they were surrounded by Angie and Willie's friends wishing them well in future endeavors. One by one their friends came to congratulate and invite them to their Graduation celebrations.

Tomeeka along with Lance and their parents came next and invited everyone to a barbeque at Tomeeka's house. Their backyard was equipped with a pool to die for, a Jacuzzi, and sauna. Their backyard barbeques were always the talk of the town for weeks afterwards. "We'd love to attend the barbeque. We'll go home and change. Do we need to bring anything", asked Mrs. Hill.

"No need to bring anything, my husband has enough food for the entire neighborhood", answered Tomeeka's Mother. Sharing a laugh the two ladies winked and turned their attention back to the matter at hand.

Angie rode home with her parents, and nearly fainted when they drove up to the house. There parked in the driveway was a brand new, shiny, red, Cruiser.

Laughing aloud at their daughter's reaction her father stated, "Well I guess that means you like your graduation gift.

"Like it, I love it", declared Angie as she opened the door to her parent's car. Springing forth, she ran to the car and ran her hands over every inch of the exterior. Taking the keys from his pocket, her father dangled them and asked, "Want to have a look at the interior"?

"Martin, stopping stringing the girl along, give over, and hand her those keys", said a smiling Mrs. Hill.

He tossed them towards her and without missing a beat; she grabbed them out of the air and unlocked the door on the driver's side. Seating herself behind the steering wheel, she gave a squeal of delight. "Thank You, Mom and Dad, aw man Meeka's gonna flip when she sees this."

Just then they turned to the squeals of delight coming from Meeka's house as she drove up and looked at Angie's gift.

Running over she got in to the passenger side, talking a mile a minute. "It's gorgeous Angie."

"I know, isn't it just the bomb", Angie asked her friend. One by one Angie and Tomeeka's friends gravitated over to the Hill home to take a look at Angie's Graduation present. All afternoon there was a steady stream between the two homes as word got around that Angie had a new car.

Willie smiled and took a look at the car along with Mitchell and Lance. After looking it over he said simply, "Congrats, it's a nice car."

"Thanks, Mom says that Dad wouldn't settle for anything less, knowing how much I liked these cars. She says they drove all the way to Carson City to pick it out", Angie said excitedly.

"Man, your Pops is a trip Angie", remarked Lance. They all laughed in agreement and walked over to Tomeeka's for the barbeque. Willie held Angie back slightly and waited for the others to enter the backyard before stopping. Pulling a small box from his pocket, he handed it to Angie by saying; "This is from me to you."

Angie slowly opened the box, having no idea what it could contain. A smile broke out across her face as she spied the prettiest heart shaped necklace she'd ever seen. On one side the words, "My Friend was printed, and on the other there was a small passage about that friendship. Looking at him through tear-laden eyes, she hugged him tightly and said, "Come on I have something for you as well." Taking hold of his hand she led him back across the street towards her home.

Her parents were still there and she left Willie in the family room with them, as she went upstairs to retrieve his graduation gift. Returning quickly she handed him the small package and watched as he opened the box and promptly burst into laughter.

Their gifts complemented each other perfectly. Willie picked up the brass heart- shaped key ring and looked at the half he held in his hand. His half read, Frie, and Alw. Angie's half read, nds, ays. Put together they read, Friends Always.

Her parent's made their way to the kitchen and waited for a few minutes, leaving the young couple to have some brief time alone. After about twenty minutes, Angie heard her father call out, "Hey guys, I don't know about you, but that barbeque is calling my name."

Knowing that their time alone was promptly over, the two stood and walked towards the kitchen. Smiling, Willie, said, "I know what you mean Mr. Hill, I think it just whispered my name as well." Just then his stomach growled as in affirmation, causing them all to laugh. Unable to resist, Mr. Hill added, "No son that's not a whisper, but rather a growl", causing everyone to laugh aloud again.

A Woman of Honor; A Child of God

In Love with my Friend

In love with my friend, I'm in love with my friend
But when did this begin?
For the first time ever, I saw your face today
In a new light, I see you now in a different way.
Your eyes speak to my soul
Finally I feel as if I've been made whole.
I ask myself, is this really love?
And then I thank God up above.
He knew I needed you
No one else would do.
Only You my friend
Could God truly depend!
He gave me a love so true
When He gave me you.
With you by my side, I can fulfill my destiny
God had it all planned when he created you and me.
In Love with my friend, I'm in love with my friend
Because our love grew from deep within.

Melissa Ann Ross

Chapter Twenty-three

The time for Angie to leave for campus came quicker than expected and her Mother and Father found it harder than they'd imagined. Swiping away at the tears falling from the corners of her eyes, Mrs. Hill, said bravely, "Well young lady, we leave you to do your unpacking and settling in."

Stepping away she nudged her husband in Angie's direction and smiled in encouragement.

Taking his baby girl into his arms, Mr. Hill whispered, "We're only a phone call away."

Shaking her head in agreement, Angie finally managed to say, "I know Dad." Gathering more courage she added, "You two had better get back on the road, night is fast approaching."

Agreeing with her daughter and anxious to get to the car before the tears fell in earnesty, Mrs. Hill placed her hand on her husband's forearm and said, "Let's go dear, Angie needs to get some unpacking done and some time to meet with her friends."

Taking a reluctant step towards the door, Mr. Hill said once more, "Remember, just a phone call away."

Swallowing the lump in her throat, Angie blinked away the shimmering tears, and wished them a safe trip, "Be careful on the way home, and call me on my cell when you make it in ok."

"Sure sweetpea, we'll call you when we reach home", her mother said as she kissed her daughter goodbye once more.

Unable to do so without breaking down, her father simply walked from the room and waited outside the door as his wife joined him. Noticing that Angie was preparing to go downstairs with them, Mrs. Hill, said quickly, "No dear, you stay here, we'll be fine, besides, you don't want your new roommate to be greeted by all of this."

"Right, you're right Mom, don't want her to think I'm a slob or something, well talk to you later", Angie said as bravely as she could.

Knowing that her daughter or husband didn't have the strength to do so, Mrs. Hill pulled the door shut and led her husband down the hallway to the exit.

Angie felt as if she were saying goodbye for the last time and nearly ran to the door to stop them from leaving. Stopping herself she said aloud, "Girl, get it together, you'll see them in a couple of weeks." She began telling herself that this was the beginning of a new life; today she was becoming an adult. Only thoughts of being able to spend uninterrupted time with Willie brought a real smile to her face. Willie she suddenly remembered had been here for three weeks already for football practice. She found his number and called him up, "Hey Willie it's me, Angie."

Knowing what she was going through, he told her to get in her car and drive over to Seibert Dorms, "Take a right on Broad, and then a left on University lane, Seibert dorms will be on your right, and I'll be waiting for you."

"Thanks Willie", she muttered with a heavy heart.

"Hey, You my girl", came the reply.

A Woman of Honor; A Child of God

Willie took one look at her face and opened his arms, saying, "What you need is a hug."

Walking into his arms, she let go of all the emotions she'd been holding in check since her parent's departure. After she cried until the well was dry, Willie took her to see a movie, and to dinner.

That night marked the new beginning of a different kind of relationship for Willie and Angie. You rarely saw one without the other from that day forward. On weekends they came home to see their parent's and attend church.

Everyone began to think of them as a couple and treated them as such, including their parents. As semester after semester passed by their attachment to one another grew stronger and stronger, leaving doubt in no one's mind that they were truly committed to one another.

During their junior year Willie announced to everyone that he was accepting his call into the ministry. Angie was so proud of him, and even studied with him as he prepared his trial sermon.

That Sunday as he entered the pulpit, she felt as though her heart would burst with pride. Standing before everyone with a word from God, was her Willie. Her friend, her confidant, her pal, Her Willie, was now a true servant of God. Thinking of how she had almost never gotten to know him, she thanked God again and then stood as Willie began to read Romans 10:1-17 verses.

Angie stood and walked to the front of the church at the end of service. Willie spied her long before she made it to his side and winked slightly. She waited as members of the congregation congratulated him on job well done. She smiled a little brighter as Deacon Gilliam shook Willie's hand. She waited along with everyone else as he commented, "Mighty good job there young man, you just continue to let the Lord use you."

Several gasps were heard at this pronouncement; Deacon Gilliam never had anything good to say about the sermons anyone preached, including Pastor's. Shaking his hand Willie said, "That I will Deacon Gilliam, that I will."

Afterwards Angie and her parent's went to a congratulatory dinner with Willie and his parents along with the entire Ministerial Staff and their families.

Pastor presented Willie with the standard Study Bible the church gave to all of its new Ministers. Clearing his throat he said, "I'd like to take this opportunity to present this Bible to Minister William Dillard. I'd also like to encourage you to keep your hand in God's hand and to follow where leads."

Accepting the gift Willie stood and said, "Thank you Pastor for all of your support, I ask simply that all of you keep me in your prayers."

Taking his seat once again they all turned their attention to the menu and selected their meals. Angie and Willie spoke quietly and laughed occasionally. Her Mother looked at her father knowingly and smiled, while giving his hand a secret squeeze under the table. She knew that each time Angie smiled at Willie, her father thought of the day that she would start a new life at the young man's side. Just yesterday her husband had brought up the subject again. "Honey", he'd said, "I got a feeling that young man is going to ask for her hand real soon, and I don't know what I'll do." She had chuckled and said, "You'll give your consent, because to do otherwise, would break our daughter's heart into a million pieces."

Looking at the two of them now, it was hard to imagine them separately. They were perfect for each other, and everyone present knew that it was simply a matter of time before they made a lifetime commitment to one another. Everyone that is, except, Angie.

A Woman of Honor; A Child of God

Angie smiled and wondered again why Willie stayed with her. They weren't even having a sexual relationship, and they were past their teenage years. Willie never brought it up except to say that it wasn't important, but she had her doubts. The lies and betrayal of Tommy still haunted her to this day. She just didn't know if she truly believed that sex wasn't important in an adult relationship. Had Willie been sexually active before their relationship? Did he resent her for not having experience in that department? There were tons of girls who would just love to have Willie as their guy. They were just waiting for Him to look their way. No, she told herself, what she and Willie had was for real. Not only were they committed to each other; they were committed to God as a couple. *A couple*, that had a nice ring to it. A squeeze on her knee brought her back to reality. She looked up at Willie and smiled, there she read the answers to all of her questions. Willie loved and accepted her, just as she was, a Woman of Honor, a Child of God.

Chapter Twenty-four

Their wedding day dawned with all the flair of a storybook fairy tale. Angie was dressed in white lace from head to foot. The front of her bodice sported a heart cutout above a satin fitted skirt. The bodice was made out of lace and pearls. There were a total of 20 pearl and diamond buttons down her back.

Her wedding gown came with a detachable 20ft lace and pearl train. Her headpiece was a lace confection dappled with diamonds and pearls. On her feet were glass slippers and her ears were adorned in diamonds.

Her mother wiped away another errant tear as she fastened a diamond necklace around her daughter's throat. "This was my great-grandmother's. She wore it on her wedding day, my mother wore it, and I wore it when I married your father", she managed in between tearful gulps.

Tomeeka stood next and said, "Angie, you look like Cinderella." Hugging her she added, "I am so happy for you and Willie."

Hugging her friend Angie answered, "Thanks Meeka, did you ever think we'd be at my wedding first"?

Laughing everyone said, "No." "I know I didn't, I thought it would be Meeka and Lance first", said Ashley. "And I thought it would be you and A. J.", Meeka shot back.

"Well, so much for that thought", answered Ashley. Placing her hand on the young woman's shoulder Mrs. Hill said, "Don't worry Ashley I'm sure you'll find that special someone."

"I'm not worried Mrs. Hill, in fact I met someone else a few weeks ago, who has made me wonder if A. J. ever even existed", replied Ashley.

"What", "You dating somebody girlfriend", asked Angie.

"A new man, fess up girlfriend" this from Felicia who was having the finishing touches added as the stylist did her hair.

Taking this as her cue to leave to check on things, Mrs. Hill got up and said, "I'll return shortly, I just want to make sure that everything is going according to plan."

"Sure Mom", called out Angie as she turned her attention back to Ashley.

The knock came on the door at just past 3:00pm and they all hugged one last time as Angie prepared to marry Willie.

Finally it was time for Mr. Hill to escort Angie down the aisle of the church to meet her awaiting groom. Steeling himself for the assault of feelings he knew would rush him, he took a deep breath and smiled into his daughter's beautiful face.

"Ready, baby girl", he asked while fighting back the tears.

"I've never been more ready to do anything in my life Daddy", came the reply. He bent to kiss her cheek before pulling down her veil, but stopped as she added, "All shall be well Daddy, you and Mommy have raised me for such a day as this."

Crushing her to him he said proudly, "I Love You, Angela Nicole Hill."

Giggling she said, "Just had to say it one last time huh daddy."

"Just like your mother, always could read me", he replied as he placed her veil over her face and placed her hand in the crease of his elbow.

The church stood as they came into view and Willie got his first view of his bride. His heart did a triple flip and he was afraid it would beat right out of his chest. Gliding towards him was a vision like no other. She looked just like an angel floating down the aisle on her father's arm.

Finally they reached the fourth pew and he walked towards her and accepted her hand from her father. He shook Mr. Hill's hand and said, "Thank You for entrusting me with the care of your daughter."

"I couldn't have picked a better man to be her husband, if I'd chosen you myself", came the reply.

A tear escaped the corner of Angie's eye at that point and Willie promptly took her hand and walked to the front of the church towards their Pastor.

The day went by in a buzz of excitement. One moment they had been standing before Pastor Jenkins, and now they were alone some 5000 miles away. Their flight had taken them directly to their honeymoon destination and now here they were in Vera Cruz.

Unable to put it off any longer Angie took a deep breath and said, "Willie, I…I hope that you understand that I…"

Not letting her finish what she was about to say, Willie took her hands into his and said, "Angie, I love you, just the way you are. You are giving me a precious gift, and I am honored to receive it."

"But Willie, I…", she tried to interject.

"No Angie, listen to me, You are a Woman of Honor, a Child of God, who not only knows His word, but you're someone who lives by His word. I love and accept you just the way you are, because God called you to be who you are. He made you just for me, and me just for you."

He took her into his arms then, and kissed away all of her fears, while promising to love and cherish her all the days of his life. Letting go of all of her doubts and fears, Angie lost herself in the feelings his kisses were creating. Closing her eyes, she melted into his embrace and her new husband strove to show her just how precious she was to him.

Who can find a virtuous woman? For her price is far above rubies. The heart of her husband doth safely trust in her, so that he shall have no need of spoil. She will do him good and not evil all the days of her life. Favour is deceitful, and beauty is vain, but a woman that feareth the Lord, she shall be praised. Give her of the fruit of her hands; and let her own works praise her in the gates.
Proverbs 31:10-12,30-31

A Vow of Abstinence

I,_____, vow before my parents, and God to abstain from the sale and use of intoxicating liquors as a beverage. I vow to abstain from the use of all drugs and tobacco products. I vow to abstain from all sexual activities as commanded by God until marriage. I vow to present my body as a living sacrifice, holy, acceptable unto God, and not to be conformed to this world, but to be transformed by the renewing of my mind, so that I may prove what is good and acceptable unto God.

I vow to stand upon the word of God and to hold fast to the principles that my faith teaches. I will not be ashamed of the Gospel and will share it with those who don't know him in the pardon of their sins. I will stand boldly and proclaim him, King of Kings, and Lord of Lords. I believe in my heart and confess with my mouth that Jesus Christ is Lord and that God raised him from the dead.

I make this vow on the _____ day of _____, 20____.

_____
Signature of Teen or Young Adult

_____
Signature of Parent

_____
Signature of Parent

About The Author

Melissa Ann Ross, a Licensed Minister, has been writing for over ten years. A native of Lake Charles, Louisiana, she enjoys spending time at home with her husband and four children. Melissa met her husband Ray, while serving in the United States Army, in Honduras, Central America. When she isn't writing, she can be found studying the word of God. Melissa recently published her first novel, "*Love is Forever*", the first of a trilogy with 1st Books Library. This book, "*A Woman of Honor, A Child of God*", was a labor of love. She prays that this book will be instrumental in helping today's Teen/Young Adult Christian, to choose rightfully between God's word, and peer pressure. She wants them to know that it's ok to be different, it's ok to stand up for is right in the sight of God.

Printed in the United States
66479LVS00001B/184-210